Anne Is Elegant

Anne Is Elegant

Mary Louise Cuneo

HarperCollins*Publishers*

Library of Congress Cataloging-in-Publication Data
Cuneo, Mary Louise.
    Anne is elegant / Mary Louise Cuneo.
        p.   cm.
    Summary: Growing up in Chicago in 1936, twelve-year-old Anna must
cope with the emotional impact of the death of her infant brother.
    ISBN 0-06-022992-6. — ISBN 0-06-022993-4 (lib. bdg.)
    [1. Death—Fiction.   2. Family problems—Fiction.   3. Chicago (Ill.)—
Fiction.]   I. Title.
PZ7.C91615An   1993   92-42417
[Fic]—dc20   .   CIP
                                                                      AC

Typography by Tom Starace
1   2   3   4   5   6   7   8   9   10

First Edition

For my mother,
who offered everyone years of such elegant
things as courage and laughter

One

Aunt Maria's apartment was like a small part of a castle, saved and brought to the city.

Anna loved it. She could have sat on the curved window seat in the living room of the apartment forever, looking down from the height, four stories up.

In the shops below, across the street, lights began to come on as the December dusk fell. Cars moved along the street in a simple, uncrowded, reliable pattern.

Later on, the street would be empty. The shops would be closed. Everything would be quiet. Blackness would fill all the rooms up here as Aunt Maria and Grandmother Schwann slept.

Anna had never been in the apartment all night long, sleeping there. Aunt Maria was not her real aunt, and Grandmother was not her grandmother. They were Priscilla's.

Priscilla's parents weren't Anna's uncle and aunt either. But she had always called them Uncle Charles and Aunt Eleanor.

Anna thought that her family was like a geometry compass opening as far as it could go. The top was the long-ago German immigrant who was everybody's ancestor. The legs at the separated sharp tips were her father and Priscilla's father.

There was no important place among the distant Schwanns for Anna. But she did have a tacked-on place. She was supposed to be Priscilla Schwann's best friend—because of the compass, and because they lived across the street from each other and were the same age, seventh graders now.

The good part of being related like this to Priscilla was visiting Aunt Maria's apartment when Priscilla and her parents visited. It was always a Sunday visit. It was always for dinner, summer and winter.

Anna liked winter better—this present remote moment of silent street-level happenings, like the slow end of a book. It was a comforting moment. Aunt Maria's apartment was collecting itself against things like bad dreams, not allowing them at night any more than it allowed them during the day.

Anna knew about things like bad dreams.

She scraped her teeth over her bottom lip. She concentrated on one car, gliding up to the corner.

"I'm back," Priscilla said loudly. "My mother says you should go to the bathroom now. We're leaving pretty soon."

Anna turned her face away.

"Use the hall bathroom," Priscilla continued, not noticing. "Grandmother's sicker, and flushing the other toilet would wake her up."

This time, Anna thought, *There must be a million nicer ways to say a thing like that. Priscilla makes it sound like toilet recess when you're in kindergarten.*

When Anna came out of the hall bathroom, Priscilla called to her, "We're over here."

Nobody said, "Hush, Priscilla. Grandmother's sleeping."

Priscilla, her father and mother, and Aunt Maria were gathered near the front door. Priscilla was standing in front of a large, funny piece of furniture, which Aunt Maria called the hall tree. The hall tree looked like the picture of a giant's chair. The chair back was a heavy mirror. The chair seat was a hinged shelf. It opened onto a deep wooden box where galoshes could be kept. There were two wooden coat hooks, like an old man's fingers, on each side of the mirror's frame.

The hinged shelf was closed as usual, and a white opened box was on it, together with tissue paper and the torn wrappings of a Christmas present.

Priscilla was wearing a new knitted scarf around

her neck, on the outside of her coat. She was fussing with a hat that matched the scarf, watching herself and her new things in the mirror.

"Tuck your hair into the hat, why don't you? And pull it down over your ears." Aunt Maria sounded a little worried. "And I think the scarf would do more good on the inside."

"She's fine as she is," Priscilla's mother said. "She can always turn up her collar and—"

"Let's get going," Priscilla's father interrupted sharply. He added, "You're going to take the box, aren't you?"

"What do we want that for?" Priscilla's mother asked.

"To put the stuff back in. Until Christmas."

"Please, Charles, let her have them now. It's real December cold tonight." That was Aunt Maria, in her nice creaky voice.

"Priscilla was uncomfortable on the way here, Charles." Aunt Eleanor was setting each word out super-politely. "That's what made Maria think of giving her this Christmas present right now."

"Leave the box, then. I don't care."

Anna hurried with her jacket.

"Good-bye, Maria," Priscilla's father said. "Call right away if there's anything about Mother."

"Oh, I will, Charles," said Aunt Maria.

"Come on, girls," said Priscilla's mother. "It was a lovely dinner, Maria."

Priscilla said it, too. "It was a lovely dinner." She

kissed her aunt clumsily.

"Thank you for having me, Aunt Maria," Anna said softly. "I had a beautiful time."

Aunt Maria smiled. "I'm always glad when you come," she said—softly, too.

◆　　◆　　◆

In the backseat of the new car, Anna and Priscilla shared the plaid blanket. They could hear the heater *hemm*ing on high from the front, and it was a warm sound. But not much of the heat got all the way to them, over the high back of the front seat and across the leg-stretching space where the two jump seats were folded into the floor.

There is so much new polish on this car, Anna thought. *You can just feel people looking at us. Here we go, rolling along in The Schwannmobile. I wonder what The Schwannmobile says to ordinary cars? "Hah! I'm a 1937 Buick. You're all stuck in 1936. You can never catch all the way up."*

In the chilly back of the big new-smelling Schwannmobile, Anna smiled.

"Is it cold back there, girls?" Priscilla's mother didn't expect them to answer.

"Do you like my new scarf set?" Priscilla asked Anna.

"Sure. I like lots of colors mixed up together like that."

"It's mostly blue," Priscilla declared. "You know what? I think my mother picked it out."

"No, she didn't," Anna said instantly. "Aunt Maria picked it out."

"That's a silly thing to say. You don't know."

"Priscilla! Look at the lights on the Pier!"

"Sit still. You're pulling the blanket off," Priscilla complained. "We always see those lights."

The Schwannmobile had turned onto the drive that followed the lake shore.

For the first few seconds, the last buildings of the downtown were always the right-side land-scape. They were pretty enough, with their lights flecked against the darkness. But their prettiness was a dime-store thing compared to the Pier. The big Pier stretched out until its sparkling far end made a nighttime horizon of its own. Two strings of gigantic light bulbs outlined the entire structure.

Anna sighed. *Look at the Pier, Priscilla. Just look.* Anna probably wiggled.

"Anna, could you just please try to sit still? You make a cold breeze when you wiggle." Priscilla was silent for a second, then whispered in Anna's direction, "Do you have to go to the toilet?"

Kindergarten. Again.

The Pier passed. Anna settled back.

Aunt Eleanor turned her head. Over her shoulder, she said, "Anna, I want to come over tomorrow afternoon. I want to take your mother for a nice ride in the new car. Will you be sure to be there right after school? Michael will be napping then, won't he? Priscilla can help."

"I think so, Aunt Eleanor," Anna answered uncertainly. "He might not be asleep. But that's all right."

Uncle Charles said something Anna couldn't hear.

Aunt Eleanor answered him clearly. "Of course not, if there's a blizzard."

"I wonder where they'll go." Priscilla was whispering again. "Maybe downtown. To cheer your mother up."

It took just those seconds of Schwann talk to make Anna feel frightened and hollow.

She knew how things would happen tomorrow afternoon. Priscilla and Aunt Eleanor would easily cross Hunt Street to Anna's house, without any worries at all. There, Anna would be taking care of Michael, who was three. And Anna's mother would be getting ready to take her sorrow with her for her great ride in The Schwannmobile.

It was now six months since Johnny Halder died. Their baby. Anna's baby brother. He hadn't even been half a year old. But he had undeniably had black hair and white skin and big round blue eyes. And he undeniably couldn't get better when he got sick in the last terribly hot, still, perfectly ordinary July.

Anna's mother couldn't forget anything about Johnny's dying. That coiled itself into the thing like a bad dream that was always waiting for Anna.

"Don't you wonder where they'll go?" Priscilla's whisper was insistent.

Anna didn't answer. She was trying to think hard about Aunt Maria's wide windows, with the small streetlights below and the safe little shops.

If she thought hard about something as good as that, Anna knew, she could fill her head with the calmness of it, and shut off her inside hearing. The words people said were only outside sounds, if she did it right. The thing that was like a bad dream could not catch Anna then.

Anna didn't want to pay attention to Priscilla's whispers because she was afraid she would cry— although she had never cried yet—right there, in front of Priscilla's white face.

Another whisper. "Anna, I asked you where you think they'll go to cheer your mother up."

Anna heard all of Priscilla's words. Thinking hard wasn't helping her this time.

She said, "I don't know."

"Does your mother still cry a lot?"

Anna drew in her breath. "No!" she answered.

She added a lie because she had to—to turn Priscilla away from this questioning. "We're making Christmas cookies."

It didn't work. Priscilla insisted, "She could still cry."

"Who wants wet cookies?"

Priscilla gasped. "Anna Halder, I think you're terrible!"

"Girls, don't fight." Aunt Eleanor said that automatically.

They didn't fight. For a long time, they didn't talk either.

The car was getting closer to home.

Finally, Priscilla turned to Anna, with something she really needed to whisper. "I think they're going to give me high-top boots for Christmas. Maybe with a knife pocket. But I won't keep a knife in it. I think I'd be warmer with high-tops."

"I guess so. Everybody is."

The Schwannmobile turned off the well-lit drive into the neighborhood of narrow streets.

It was very quiet. The new car glided politely along until it came to the Schwann house, with the Halder house waiting across the street. The Schwannmobile stopped.

Priscilla took the blanket. She wrapped it around her shoulders and pushed the door open with her blanket-shoulder.

Uncle Charles walked across the street with Anna. He always did—in summer heat waves, in winter freezes. He never said a thing to her. He just continued. He preceded her up the steps. He rang the Halder front-door bell himself.

Tonight Uncle Charles came into the house. He didn't always. He kept his coat, but took off his galoshes. In some way that had escaped Anna's noticing, her father had taken Uncle Charles' hat. Her father sat down, holding the hat.

Uncle Charles, in his coat, sat down, too. He looked, Anna thought, as though he had been lowered from the top into the big coat, and he was sitting in it stiffly and seriously.

Uncle Charles' hat was a stiff and serious hat. In her father's hands right now—Anna suddenly fretted—could the hat turn into a tease, her father being a good teaser? *"Do we lower the hat from the top too, Charles?" No! My father doesn't tease Uncle Charles. But what if he did, for once? It would be embarrassing.*

It wouldn't be the kind of teasing Anna always liked, which was fun for someone like Anna. But not Uncle Charles.

Why am I thinking about this dumb thing at all! I've got teasing on the brain.

Her father now asked quietly, "How is Grandmother, Charles?"

"There's some change, Justin," Uncle Charles answered. "Not much. We're prepared, Maria and I. And Eleanor. It's Mother's years. She's holding on. But it's the years."

She's going to die.

Anna's father looked down at the hat. Still standing uncertainly at the door of the living room, Anna knew something in a minute. Her father was thinking about Grandmother's years and Grandmother's dying. Johnny's dying was there in the living room with Anna's father.

Uncle Charles cleared his throat. "It's a mean night," he offered.

In the silent space after that comment, Anna had a chance to say, "Thank you for taking me, Uncle Charles. I have to go upstairs now. I have homework."

Uncle Charles nodded.

As Anna left, he was continuing, "Record cold this winter. Wouldn't surprise me if it went to thirty below one of these nights. We have to suffer through it. The winters are getting worse. Bitter cold."

When she finished her homework, Anna doodled on a piece of scrap paper. Then through the territory of the round-eyed doodle faces, she wrote, *I wish he would. I wish my father would tease. I wish he would. Again. Tease.*

Anna knew now that it was one more thing changed. Her father hadn't teased since Johnny died. He never talked about Johnny. But he wasn't teasing at all now.

Two

Bitter cold.

When Anna got up the next morning, she remembered that whole, complete with the frozen sound of Uncle Charles' voice.

The furnace was engaged in its early morning huffing. There was a biting, oily smell in the cold air. Heat was blowing straight up through the register in the floor, but Anna's room wasn't occupied with warmth. Anna stood on the register as often as she could while she was getting dressed.

The kitchen, however, was fine. Everything there was warm. Michael was eating his breakfast. Anna's mother was saying, "Here comes Anna now, Michael."

"Anna!" Michael pointed with his toast. "You're going to school. Me, too. By myself."

"You'll be the neatest kid there."

Every day at breakfast, Michael was shiny. His

straight hair was as light as fairy-tale straw that could be turned into gold. His brown eyes were so involved with Michael-in-the-morning sparkle that they looked almost black.

Anna gave her mother an over-the-shoulders hug. Her mother patted Anna's hand. She said, "Daddy had to leave early again."

Anna didn't ask why. There had been so many mornings like this one. She was pretty sure, now, that she knew why. It was simply easier for her father not to sit at breakfast, where anyone might be reminded about Johnny—who used to be there. Easier for him—as often as he could—to be at the quiet early office, with his pages and pages of difficult words.

Anna and her long-ago best friend Laurette had tried once—in the summer before fifth grade—to read out loud a line on a long printed page of lawyers' words. They didn't finish even the single line. "They're words, okay, Anna. But they're dumb. Does your father talk like that sometimes?"

Lately, a long time after Laurette asked the question, Anna was answering it this way for herself. *He talks like a regular father. I like the way he talks. When he's around, to talk. He's not around for breakfast now. He's in the office, peacefully fighting with the pages and pages of words.*

Anna stood up. She went over to Michael. She kissed him lightly on the top of his head.

"What do you think, Mikey?" she asked.

"Should I wear my jacket this morning?"

"No-o-o!" said Michael.

"Don't take Michael's advice, Anna."

"I'll just eat a lot of hot breakfast."

"That's a good start," said her mother.

"I eat toast!" Michael crowed.

"You're a great toast eater," Anna told him.

"Michael's a great everything," her mother said. Anna and her mother smiled.

Anna asked, "What would we do without Michael in the morning?"

It crossed her mind immediately: *We are doing without Johnny in the morning. We're doing without Daddy in the morning.* Anna felt the hollow connection between the two. She shook her head, quickly and jerkily.

But her mother was saying calmly, "It's nice when Daddy can be here for breakfast too."

Anna finished her breakfast. "I have to go now, Michael."

"No," said Michael.

"He's a great no-sayer, too," Anna's mother commented.

Anna kissed Michael again, on the top of his head. She leaned down to kiss her mother's cheek. "'Bye."

"Good-bye, darling," said her mother.

Outside, in the bright cold, Anna stepped up from the shoveled path onto the mound of dirty snow that ran along the edge of the sidewalk. It had a sturdy ice crust. Each galosh step broke into the crust and was supported there as firmly as a peg in a giant raggedy hole.

Anna's steps felt solid and crunchy. She was watching them and listening to their sound, like notebook paper crackling.

Stepping and watching and listening, Anna thought about her mother and Michael—still sitting in the warm kitchen, her mother still glad to be there with Michael, maybe finding Michael boy enough just now, maybe not remembering Johnny for a while.

Why is she happy now? Why will she cry, and talk about Johnny again—that awful talk—whenever she does? And my father is never there to listen.

From across the street came Priscilla's yell, erasing the paper sound and Anna's wondering about her mother and her father. Priscilla was waiting for her ride to the public school.

"Anna! Hey! I'll see you this afternoon. So your mother can go for a ride in our car. Don't forget!"

Anna didn't turn her head. She just nodded, up and down.

✦　　✦　　✦

The last Monday before Christmas vacation was part of a caroling, nice-smelling, rare, twirled-around time.

But Sister Elizabeth was a serious teacher.

Anna's class had to begin the day as seriously as ever—with history.

They were studying the World War. The war was close to 1936, and it was real to Anna because her parents had lived through it and talked about it.

Anna could imagine the trenches of the war, where soldiers lived in mud and hid down in it. She could imagine guns shaking the sky. She could imagine how people in cities and towns and countrysides gave up, and let war happen to them, finally just deciding to hide or to run as best as they could, and to save some little special things from the peace they had once—before trenches and mud and guns.

Anna could easily think of little possible things to save from war, but she never could do any easy imagining about Germany's ruler, the Kaiser. In the history book, there was a picture of him wearing his powerful uniform and his spiked helmet. Anna had seen that picture before—before seventh-grade history class.

The Kaiser had started the Great War, and the war had killed millions of people. There were stories about German horrors—German soldiers killing old people and babies.

With the Kaiser knowing and not caring? That would work, maybe, if he were only a kaiser, but he was a man, too. He must have done things like putting sugar in his coffee, and reading, and watching rain through a palace window. All those things, without thinking about the babies his soldiers killed?

Anna never got anywhere trying to put The Man and The Kaiser together.

Today, the Kaiser was again part of the history lesson.

Sister Elizabeth taught in little snatches. She waited while the class made notes. She asked questions. Then she closed her history book and started to talk about something as though she were remembering it.

Sister Elizabeth, who was an old lady *(about as old as Aunt Maria)*, was talking calmly about the Kaiser's family. *His family.* As though, Anna marveled, it were an ordinary family.

In the last century, when the Kaiser was born, his family was ashamed of him. They were ashamed because the new baby had a crippled arm. His grandmother was the Queen of England. His mother was going to be the Empress of Germany. They, and everyone else who knew about the arm, tried to keep it a secret.

As though the baby had done a terrible thing himself.

"It's an interesting footnote to history," Sister Elizabeth finished. She announced, "Civics."

Civics didn't need much thought. Mechanically, Anna filled in the blanks in the workbook. There was a lot of pencil scratching, but the room was quiet around it.

Anna hadn't stopped thinking about the crippled

arm. The crippled Kaiser had spent some time being three years old, Michael's age.

What could I possibly say to Michael? "I love you. Don't worry. There are still a million things you can do."

What million things, exactly?

Did the baby Kaiser's arm hurt?

At odd times during the rest of the morning, and even in the lunchroom later, Anna wondered. It was like being forced to pay attention to a paper cut.

Something about paper cuts made Anna, sitting in the required lunchroom silence, think about Laurette. Laurette would have cared about the baby Kaiser, but she wouldn't have stood for the paper-cut feeling. She would have said to Anna, "You're not supposed to be sad about everybody, Anna."

Last year, in the sixth grade, Laurette was a lot shorter than Anna. *She's probably still shorter than me, in Canada. She probably still looks like she's made with little sticks glued together.*

Laurette's mother wasn't much bigger than Laurette. She did beautiful embroidery, probably—Anna had decided—all day long. That left Laurette to take care of some practical things, such as being sure that there was enough bread in the house.

"But yes," her mother would say from the sofa, with the silk colors around her. She would say it as though it were a very good and nice idea that Laurette had just had—as though not many people thought about bread, particularly if they could feel silk threads on their fingertips. "Yes, little Laurette and little Anna," she would continue with a smile. "Take a dime and buy a bread."

There was a good shortcut from Laurette's house to the grocery store. It led down a wide, neat alley that was public, and then along a sidewalk that really belonged only to a private apartment building. Anna was uneasy there—not belonging—but Laurette never needed to hurry. She always kept talking. Anna would be glad when they finished on that sidewalk, but she talked, too.

Suddenly, a while before Laurette moved, the talk—on that private and empty and kind of spooky sidewalk—was about boys. Laurette started the talk, surprising Anna one day by saying, "I like George Farley. I'll tell you why. Because he's smart and he's kind of dumb, too."

From then on, considering George Farley became part—just a part—of the bread walks that remained, with Laurette saying things like "Some of the dumb part about George is that he's so loud. He doesn't have to be that loud. Anna, do you think he's handsome?"

When Anna answered that she did—or answered any other George Farley question—there were then other things to talk about.

Maybe Anna was being scared, in a way. She

never did tell Laurette what boy she liked, and try to tell Laurette why.

Anna had thought so often, about Laurette and her mother, *I wish they didn't move,* that she didn't think it in words anymore. Being lonesome for them was just there, set in a place in her mind.

After lunch, the day droned on. Laurette, and wondering about the baby Kaiser, settled away in the back of Anna's mind.

"Literature."

The last class of the day was Anna's favorite. Nothing about literature ever seemed like work to her. The droning day turned light and interesting.

It was a class assignment to memorize "To a Waterfowl." Each person had to recite the poem, sometime before January exams, for Sister Elizabeth.

Anna had recited the poem already. Marianne Grimes and Leo McVene were ready today.

Anna really did like to listen to the poem. But then it was Leo's turn, and Anna didn't know what to do. It was polite to look at the reciter. Anna couldn't look, directly—her full face hanging unmasked in the dull, overheated late-afternoon air of the classroom—at Leo McVene.

Priscilla had once said that Leo McVene was "peachy-darn-good-looking." Priscilla said that about Anna's father, too. It didn't mean much, coming from Priscilla. But Leo McVene did mean something to Anna. She didn't know what to do with it. Wish that it wasn't there and wish that it was there all the time?

Anna sighed, and wondered with instant embarrassment if Sister Elizabeth had looked up at the sigh.

Sister was listening to Leo and correcting arithmetic papers at the same time, her red pencil-top bouncing along. Anna concentrated on Sister's bowed head, her boxed black bonnet tipped downward.

When Leo finished, Sister said, looking up, "Excellent." She continued, "Please remain standing, Leo. You may read the first poem in the next section of the text. That will get us started on our new work. We'll be ready for January."

Leo reached down for his book. Right along with him, all the rest of the class turned pages. It sounded like a strong breeze blowing up and then dying down.

Leo skipped the title of the poem—"Little Boy Blue." Anna was looking down at her text.

Leo began the first lines.

> The little toy dog is covered with dust,
> But sturdy and staunch he stands;
> And the little toy soldier is red with rust,
> And his musket moulds in his hands. . . .

It went on to the end. It was about the little boy who owned the toys and left them behind when he died. Anna absorbed this quickly because she read through the whole poem while Leo was edging himself along those first lines.

Anna stared at the page. She would have said that there wasn't a sound of any movement in the whole classroom. She kept on staring.

If I look up, will I see that everyone is looking at me? Wondering how I feel to be reminded that a little boy died?

Anna tried to get back to Aunt Maria's apartment, thinking hard about its protectingness.

Sister Elizabeth said abruptly, "Stop."

Anna looked up, startled away from the apartment, and scared. But Sister didn't mean her. Sister continued calmly, to Leo. "Stop, Leo, please. That's enough of that. I didn't remember that that particular poem came next. Some things we can skip."

She told the class to clear their desks. "We're going to sing Christmas carols," she said. Sister Elizabeth's total gathered-together cheerfulness made that announcement come out loud, very loud for an old nun.

Sister never sounds that cheerful . . . never. Anna's whole face felt too tight. For the first time in her life, Anna listened to Christmas carols and didn't feel anything special.

Laurette wasn't there anymore, and everybody else left Anna alone. No one told her now to sing, too. Anna was different. Anna would always be different. Because of Johnny.

When class was dismissed for the day, Anna ducked away without talking to anyone.

On the way home, she was far ahead of every-body.

The street looked cold, gray—and empty and unfriendly at the same time. Nothing was moving except an uninteresting, dissatisfied winter wind. When it picked up in sharpened instants, it complained, and reminded Anna of Uncle Charles.

An Uncle Charles complaining wind. And when I get home, there'll be Priscilla, the same Priscilla. Priscilla isn't great to have around on a bad day.

Anna's galoshes were getting heavy. One galosh thump agreed that Sister Elizabeth had stopped Leo's reading because of her, because Johnny had died. The other thump argued that nobody—not even Sister Elizabeth, who was supposed to think that it was great to die and go to God—remembered anything about Johnny.

Which was better? Anna swallowed in her sort of swollen throat. She didn't know.

Running feet were suddenly pounding the sidewalk behind her.

"GANGWAY!"

George Farley ran past Anna on the sidewalk. He poked out his elbow but missed her. Leo McVene was right behind George. He ran, looking straight ahead. *He probably doesn't notice that I'm here, in my galoshes.*

"Onward! To Clark Hill!" George Farley was yelling. "Everybody meet at Clark Hill!"

They kept running. Anna watched them go.

They'd run home, get their sleds, then run some more—to Clark Hill. It was a big hill, steep, and perfect for sledding. Most of the seventh grade—from both schools, Catholic and public—would be there today. All the sixth graders and younger kids who were allowed to come would be there, and the eighth graders who didn't pretend that sledding was babyish.

Anna loved everything about sledding. She even loved it when her legs got chapped where her snow-wet woolen snow pants rubbed on them while she was walking home. That was a part of sledding—the final joy of rubbing lotion on stings. To have flown on the hill, to be blissfully tired and warm from the inside out, and then to be soothed with almond lotion like a perfume she had inherited. That was the beautiful way sledding ended for Anna.

Here go my galoshes, slopping onward. I'm not going sledding. I'm going Priscilla-ing.

Anna was walking slowly now. She was planning a daydream to substitute for sledding. She was stepping into the daydream.

Walking down the street toward Aunt Maria's. There is time to stop in the shops along the way. Leo McVene, who is with me, wonders why I like certain things in the shops so much. We're going together to Aunt Maria's apartment.

Anna reached the corner of Hunt Street. It was not a daydream. It was real. And now it looked empty. She saw that there was no Schwannmobile parked at the Schwannmobile curb.

She had an instant mixed-up feeling—one part guilt, one part confusion. *I wasted too much time. Why did they have to go before I got here?*

Priscilla would be staying with Michael. That would be, Anna was sure, pretty hard on Priscilla.

This is crazy. It was supposed to be a Schwann-mobile ride, any old time. I wonder if Aunt Eleanor decided to take Mother to a matinee?

A little Schwannmobile ride? And then a lot of cheering up at the movies? Was that what Aunt Eleanor was in charge of now, for Anna's mother?

Three

The back door was unlocked, as usual.

Anna sat down on the stairs to yank off her galoshes. She threw them on the rug scrap in the corner. She hurried up the steps.

Her mother was in the living room, sitting at the small square telephone table in the corner. She was holding one folded hand to her mouth, lightly and thoughtfully, as though she were deciding to suck—or not to suck—her thumb.

"Mother?"

Her mother lowered her hand. "Anna. Aunt Eleanor called. Grandmother died a little while ago. They're at Maria's now. Daddy too."

"Oh! Poor Aunt Maria!"

"Grandmother died in her sleep, Anna."

Michael started to cry, from his room upstairs. It was after-nap sobbing, not a usual thing with Michael.

"Will you go to him, Anna, please?"

Going up to Michael, Anna passed Johnny's picture on the staircase wall. It was there with everybody else's picture. It was definitely a nice picture of a nice little baby.

But . . . will it combine with Grandmother's old death, and start the terrible talk again—right now—about baby death?

Michael was standing at the safety gate stretched across the doorway of his room. It was a good gate. It kept Michael safe in a little country of his own, protected, just as such a small person ought to be.

"Hello, old Michael."

Anna let him out of his little country and gave him a hug. Her face got wet with his tears. He snuggled for a couple of minutes and, when he pulled back, crying was over and done. "Now I can get up. I can get up, Anna?"

When they got downstairs together, their mother was still sitting at the telephone table. Michael climbed into her lap. He fit himself into the bend of her arm.

"Anna, it's silly that I'm still right here. After I called Daddy, I started trying to think of other people to call, to tell about Aunt Rose. But Anna, there is no one else. I can't think of anyone else who is still alive. Daddy was the only one to call."

Don't talk about old dead people. Please don't.

Her mother started playing with Michael's

sleepy fingers, moving them gently, then folding his little fist inside her hand.

"Years ago, there would have been so many people. Even after Uncle Philip died. Aunt Rose was a natural center. People gathered around her."

"Michael's going back to sleep," Anna said very softly.

"It wasn't usual for a woman to be as smart as Aunt Rose was and not try to hide it," her mother continued. "And to be as charming."

Michael stirred. His mother kissed the back of his head.

"Aunt Rose was on mayors' committees and every other sensible committee there was. Did Maria ever show you Aunt Rose's scrapbook, Anna?"

"A scrapbook? No. Not a scrapbook."

"There's a picture in there. I suppose it's still there. Of us, Daddy and me. With Charles and Eleanor. And Maria. Aunt Rose is in the middle of the picture. It was taken on the day of the engagement party she gave for us. The picture was in the paper—not because of us, but because of Aunt Rose. Aunt Rose was famous—in a nice, charming, Aunt Rose way."

Anna thought about Grandmother, when Grandmother was Aunt Rose. She said, "She was probably more like Aunt Maria."

"Oh? More like Maria than Charles. Is that what you mean, Anna?"

"Uncle Charles isn't charming, Mother."

Her mother smiled. "If Uncle Charles only ever listened to himself once, Anna, I bet he'd say, 'Is this me, Charles, talking? By George, I'm going to change. I am going to change and be charming.'"

Anna smiled back. "It wouldn't work, Mother."

Michael slid to the floor. He started off independently.

"I need you again for Michael, Anna. Will you take care of him for a while?"

"Sure."

She talked about Uncle Charles, of all people. That's good. She didn't talk about Johnny.

Anna caught up with Michael. She took his small hand. "Want to build the village?"

He watched, and bumped Anna's legs, as she got down the miniature German village from the closet shelf. It was Anna's village, from many Christmases ago. When Michael played with it, the village needed some watchful protecting. The houses and buildings were tiny and neat and exact—and highly breakable. And so were the spongy trees, and the train, and the people who fit it all.

Michael chattered like a little wound-up record. He was telling himself all the wonderful things Michael Halder, big as a builder, was doing in the little village. At the moment, Michael didn't need to talk to Anna, too. She watched him, and the village spread out around him.

Michael and his village made Anna think of *A Child's Garden of Verses*, and the way her father had read the verses to her night after night when she was little.

Michael is the giant, great and still? Still? No, not Michael.

But the boy-giant in the verse had to be still. He was ailing, and couldn't get out of bed. He laid his village out on his lumpy bedspread, his counterpane.

> I was the giant great and still
> That sits upon the pillow-hill,
> And sees before him, dale and plain,
> The pleasant land of counterpane.

Pillow-hill. That comes close to describing Grandmother's big chair, when she was sick and I used to see her. She was pale and propped up, and she didn't talk. She nodded her head almost all the time. That Grandmother just died. She floated away from her pillows. She's gone. That much is sad. But she was old. And nobody is left haunted— not any of them. Because Grandmother wasn't little. And when she did just float away, it didn't hurt her.

"No more village," Michael announced.

Anna came abruptly back to Michael, and the village, and the day. She made a game for Michael of putting each piece back where it belonged in the village crate. She always did that for Michael. She pretended that everything was gigantically heavy, heavy as a real train or tree, or a burgomaster. Michael always laughed.

✦　　✦　　✦

It was late when, long after dinner, Anna finished her homework. She came downstairs to say good night.

The living room was deeply silent, because her mother was alone. She was sitting in the biggest chair. Anna's father still wasn't home.

Anna sat down on the chair's ottoman. Her mother's eyes were frighteningly moist. She looked at Anna. "I can't believe Aunt Rose is dead, Anna. I see her moving around—little and quick, and interested in everything. You have to be alive. And you have to keep yourself young to do that— be interested in everything. That's how I go on thinking of Aunt Rose. Alive and keeping young. Isn't it sad that the young die?"

The young die. Young means baby. In a moment, Anna's mother would be talking about Johnny. Anna knew that Aunt Maria's apartment couldn't rescue her. Neither could the magical dream of Christmas shopping with Leo McVene.

Anna needed very small details to concentrate on. She needed something fussy to absorb her—to absorb her secretly while her mother talked about their baby.

This will be the same talk, about the things doctors did to him in the hospital. Where he died, probably because everything hurt him so much. I can't bear to hear about crib tents again. The babies inside are so unreal. You can't touch them or hold them. But there are needles small enough for those little babies. So somebody touches them. That's the worst thing to hear about—the needles.

The first time, unprepared, Anna heard everything. Soon, however—prepared—Anna listened, and she wasn't there. She was Anna-in-a-castle. She had princess gowns there, and they made her safe.

Anna designed each gown in her head while motionlessly she faced her mother's voice, a noise her mind wasn't hearing. Every dress, taking its turn in Anna's head, had to be changed all the time, in nearly every detail. Everything had to be hard to change. Changing had to be such a puzzle that nothing else could get inside Anna's head.

"Isn't it sad that the young die?" From there, her mother's voice continued, as Anna knew it would.

At first, with a fraction of her hearing, Anna heard about crib tents. With a pink court dress, however—a dress that required the designing of small embroidered flowers—Anna closed off the fraction and didn't hear any more.

In the matter of the sharp needles, Anna's timing was bad. Her mother's voice rushed in before Anna was ready with the new princess dress she needed.

"They told me he wouldn't feel it. But I could hear. Poor little baby."

Blue. Anna filled her head with blue—a blue dress. She was concentrating on its design. *Silver braid, like ice coating on branches in winter, when the sun is shining. That winter silver will be outlining the neckline, and the cuffs, and the hem.*

Suddenly, Anna didn't need the dress. Her mother had stopped talking.

"Anna, what a sad day," she whispered. "I didn't know I would miss Aunt Rose so much."

For a second, Anna stared at the blue gown somewhere. Then she blinked it away. Her eyelids felt thick. "I'm pretty tired, Mother."

"Go to bed, Anna. I'm going to wait for Daddy."

Anna stood. She bent down, and kissed her mother's cheek.

"Good night, Mother."

"Good night, Anna."

This remembering of Johnny was over.

On the staircase, down the hall, into her room, Anna walked slowly, thinking about it. *I wish that if Johnny had to die, he had just floated away from his pillows, too, like Grandmother—without any hurting. Then, maybe, my mother could talk about Johnny, when he was just our baby. And maybe I could talk, too. Even if we cried at first, I wouldn't sneak away with dresses. She doesn't even know that I'm sneaking away. She's bewitched, not like she usually is all the time all day long, and she just doesn't know. It's true in the old fairy tales—that someone can be bewitched. And it's so bad.*

Four

The next morning, Anna woke up from a heavy sleep with a feeling of startle, almost as terrible as panic. Something very serious was wrong. Something was the matter with the morning.

She reached for her clock. On its round lighted dial, she read eight thirty.

The next second, Anna was running down the hall. The wooden floor was as cold as a sidewalk.

"Good morning, Anna. Get your slippers. You have time."

"Mother! It's so late!"

"It doesn't matter. It's all right. I've talked to Sister Elizabeth."

"It's all right," Michael echoed from his mother's arms.

Anna's father was leaving. He said, "Anna, honey, I'm very late. I came in to talk to you last night. But you were asleep. The Schwanns need you today.

Mother will tell you."

He kissed Anna, then Michael, and was gone.

Michael said, all in one breath, "Now he is going good-bye."

His mother agreed. "Daddy's going good-bye. You're right, Michael."

Anna sat down. Her mother said, "It's so complicated to die these days, Anna. You would think that Aunt Rose would be—would have been for years and years—just a name on a file. Close it quickly, and claim all the time you want now, exclusively for missing her. But it doesn't work like that. There are so many things for Daddy to deal with."

Papers and enemy words, Anna thought.

She asked, "What did Daddy mean? What do I have to do today, with the Schwanns?"

"Aunt Eleanor needs you at the apartment, to help pack away Grandmother's things, you and Priscilla. That's what Daddy was talking about."

"Just Aunt Eleanor? Did Aunt Maria get sick?"

"No. Maria's not sick. Both of them will be packing. Aunt Eleanor is doing the heavier things, I would think. She and Uncle Charles want to get everything out quickly, for Maria's sake."

Quickly? Quickly's not Priscilla. Anna thought this instantly, with some grumpiness.

Aloud, she murmured, "At least, I'm used to Priscilla."

Her mother said lightly, "That will help."

Anna drew a deep breath. *Aunt Maria is important. I know that.* She immediately said that out loud, and added, "I really do want to help Aunt Maria."

"Good for you," her mother said. "Uncle Charles plans to leave about ten."

◆   ◆   ◆

Uncle Charles rang the front-door bell at ten o'clock exactly, with the hour striking on the Halders' small chime clock.

While Anna was still climbing into the back of The Schwannmobile, Priscilla said quaveringly, "Isn't it awful!"

Once they were underway, with car noises covering her words, Priscilla whispered, "We had to go there yesterday. I don't know why I had to go!"

"I'm glad you're going to be with us today, Anna," Aunt Eleanor said. "We'll have our hands full."

From then on, nobody talked much. The spaces between voices saying words got longer and longer. Anna thought she was getting sleepy, as though she had been up too early instead of too late.

The Pier came along. Without its lights turned on in nighttime, it was a disappointment, showing itself, as usual, to be really shabby.

The Schwannmobile turned into Aunt Maria's street and rolled toward her corner. Christmas shopping was crowded there.

Opening the door of the apartment, Aunt Maria didn't look different. "Good morning, dears," she said in her usual peering way. "Are you coming in, too, Charles?"

"There are arrangements, Maria. More funeral arrangements to see to," Uncle Charles answered. "And I'll have to get to Justin's office. No, I'm not coming in. If you don't have any problems right now . . . ?"

"No, I don't, right now," Aunt Maria said. "No problems right now, Charles."

Uncle Charles left.

In the quiet kitchen, there was hot cocoa waiting. "I thought you'd like some cocoa."

"You sit down, too, Maria," said Aunt Eleanor.

Between tastes of her cocoa, Aunt Eleanor talked. "I'll need some cardboard boxes from the basement. I'll show you girls where they are. Lord knows there are enough of them. That will be one of your big jobs today, girls. Bringing up boxes."

The entire building belonged to the Schwanns: the pretty, gracious side of the building that contained four floors of apartments, and the commercial side that met it at a right angle and continued down the far busier street where the streetcars ran. The entrance to Aunt Maria's basement was in the inner half court formed by the two arms of the building.

Now Aunt Eleanor sighed. "I still can't believe

that there's no inside entrance to the basement."
She wondered if they should go down the front
stairs, through the lobby, and out around the far
corner of the apartment building, into the courtyard. "Or climb down those rickety back stairs outside."

"They were painted last summer," Aunt Maria
said.

"I know they were painted, Maria." Aunt
Eleanor sounded precise and impatient. "Charles
had to find a painter. But paint isn't nails. I wish it
were."

"I'm sure they're safe. They've always been
safe."

Aunt Eleanor didn't comment on that. "We do
have to bring up boxes, so the shorter way is better," she said. "Maria, will you clear away the cocoa things right away? We'll need the whole
kitchen table."

"The wind is cold," said Aunt Maria. "Bundle
up."

When they got outside again, winter seemed to
be pouring up the stairs, pushing away the warmth
of Aunt Maria's cocoa. It seemed like a super-long
climb down to the basement.

"I'm freezing!" yelled Priscilla.

Aunt Eleanor unlocked the basement door.
Priscilla pushed inside in front of her mother.
There were two more keys inside for Aunt
Eleanor to deal with. They were the keys for two

separate locks on the door to Aunt Maria's slatted storage locker.

Anna thought immediately of the crate for the German village. *It's like an extra-huge crate. Oh, I like crates. I like the special places for interesting things that fit. There are hundreds of interesting things in here, I bet. And they all fit.*

At the back of the storage crate, there was a long, large table big enough for a banquet. The table was draped with canvas, which did not reach the floor. Chairs on their backs were stored on brown-paper sheets under the table. Anna saw, on the canvas surface, two matching floor-lamp poles with a brown, high chest of drawers between them. Perched on top of the tall chest was a little table by itself. It was too small and delicate and pretty to be related to any of the other mounded furniture.

Aunt Eleanor opened the second lock. She stepped back to swing the crate door open. She bumped into Anna. "I'm sorry, Anna."

"Aunt Eleanor, what's that?" Anna pointed. "It's so little, with those skinny legs. Why are they shaped like that? Oh, look, it has a drawer."

Aunt Eleanor looked up at the little table. She sighed. "That's like most of the things down here, Anna—saved, and useless. That was Maria's dressing table when she was a child. So many years ago. I'll bet it can barely stand on its legs. I wonder who would ever give a thought to that old thing again?"

Oh, I would!

"Here are the boxes," Aunt Eleanor said.

The cardboard boxes were just inside the slat door, against the left-side wooden wall. They were folded down flat and piled up. Little boxes and medium boxes and large boxes were jammed together.

"You'll have to take larger ones, girls. Take two each. You can manage two. They're not heavy, but they're extremely awkward, and those stairs are awful. I can't help. This is simply the wrong coat for carrying old dusty boxes." She looked down at her white coat.

Anna and Priscilla had to stretch their arms to hold the boxes.

"This is hard!" Priscilla complained.

Anna said, "I've carried boxes before."

"Well, I HAVEN'T! I'll take a-a-a box, one box, just one. If I take the darn two, I'll break my neck. Those are awful stairs!"

They were standing outside the locker. The slat door was closed, but not yet locked. "Be quiet a minute, girls," commanded Aunt Eleanor. "I can't figure out these keys." She jingled them impatiently. "Why won't the big one go into the big old-fashioned lock on top?" Aunt Eleanor jabbed again, and the key went in. "This old lock is too rusty," she complained. "It doesn't even count as a lock anymore. Maybe it was good enough in Grandfather's time. But in this neighborhood now, you need really good locks on everything, if you're going to survive."

Outside, this time, winter seemed to be pouring down the stairs and freezing the whole courtyard. But Aunt Eleanor said, "Wait a minute. I have to lock this door, too." She locked the outside door. She tested it by trying to turn the handle and push. She was satisfied that it was locked.

But she didn't start for the stairs. "What about the keys?" she asked. "You girls will need them again." Aunt Eleanor pulled up her collar and shivered. "Anna, you have deep pockets in that jacket. The keys should drop to the bottom."

They were three keys on a ring as big around as an apricot. Aunt Eleanor, still holding her collar, pushed them into Anna's pocket. They did drop, like a handful of rocks, to the bottom.

Now, in the cold, everyone could move.

As they were climbing the stairs, Aunt Eleanor said, "This is such an old building. Maybe it was all right when Grandfather bought it. But it's way out of date. And lots of people wouldn't want to live in this neighborhood. It's certainly slipped. It's patchy now. Shabby."

"We should have an elevator," Priscilla said.

"A smart person would sell this building before the whole neighborhood goes," her mother commented.

Anna thought of the neighborhood floating away, like a polar bear on a slab of ice. That stayed funny for a minute. But then Aunt Eleanor said,

"This building should be torn down."

Not Aunt Maria's apartment!

Aunt Eleanor finished, "There's a great deal of value in the land for development."

Aunt Maria was waiting to open the kitchen door for them. Anna and Priscilla put the three flat boxes on the table.

"Anna, you help here, with the boxes," Aunt Eleanor said. "Priscilla will be working with me in Grandmother's bedroom."

Anna's job was to hold one wobbly, newly shaped-up box upside down on the kitchen table. Aunt Maria carefully fit wet paper tape along the bottom seam. She crisscrossed the first tape with a second.

"This is the messy part, Anna." Aunt Maria pressed on the tape, ironing it along with her fingers. "But it dries fast. By the time we get to the second box, this one will be ready for Eleanor."

Before they started the second box, however, Aunt Maria decided that the first box was ready and should be delivered. Anna could have carried it alone. But Aunt Maria helped.

While they were walking down the long hall, each holding a side of the box, Aunt Maria said, "This box is so nice, and it's so pleasant to carry. If you were little, Anna, somebody could give you a ride in this box."

"They probably could, Aunt Maria. If I were little enough."

"It makes me smile," Aunt Maria said.

In Grandmother's room, Aunt Eleanor and Priscilla had stripped the big bed. The mattress was partially covered with a piece of old oilcloth, wrinkled and cracked, but still showing patterns of purple and little pink flowers. Some of Grandmother's things were set in piles on the oilcloth.

Priscilla was sitting on the edge of the chaise longue. "There's sure a lot of stuff," she said.

Anna and Aunt Maria put the box on the oilcloth. Priscilla came over and looked into it.

"We'll come with another box," Aunt Maria promised. "We'll hurry."

Anna and Aunt Maria brought the second box to Grandmother's bedroom just in time. Priscilla told them that. "You're just in time," she said. "Now we need lots of room for all the old shoes and stuff."

"Are you going to pack away all the shoes?" Aunt Maria asked anxiously. "She had such pretty dancing slippers."

"Dancing slippers? My word, Maria," said Aunt Eleanor. "We haven't seen dancing slippers. But if they're here, they've been here for sixty years."

"There are some gowns that match," Aunt Maria said. "Three whole outfits are left. Maybe we could send the gowns and the slippers to the historical society."

Aunt Eleanor sighed. "Maria, if there are gowns and slippers, they would make great costumes for parties. That's all they're good for, really. People buy that kind of thing, and the charities make money. Everything is going to the charities. We talked about it yesterday. You thought that it was fine."

"But probably not the slippers and gowns are fine. I didn't mean those. I wasn't thinking of the slippers and the gowns. Until the boxes today, and talking about Mother's shoes. I can show you the slippers in just a minute. Can't I, Anna?"

Aunt Eleanor and Priscilla turned their heads to stare at Anna. Anna's mouth was half open. She closed it and rubbed her lips together. She managed to say, "I'd like to see Grandmother's things, Aunt Maria."

Priscilla said, "You're just going to see a lot of old shoes, Anna."

Aunt Eleanor shrugged. "It can still all go to the charities sometime," she said. "I'm sure it will."

Aunt Maria beamed, as though she hadn't heard a thing. "Now we'll see the dancing slippers," she said. "We *will* try the historical society. When you see the dancing slippers, you'll know I'm right."

Aunt Maria went *(Aunt Maria danced)* to the closet. She untied a shoe bag from its hooks on the inside of the door. "These are her dancing slippers!"

Aunt Maria spaced them, in pairs, on a corner of the bed. There were seven pairs: two white, a black, and the rest in pastels. There were flower buds and small ribbons and brilliants, and even painted designs, on those slippers.

"They look like they would be dancing in a minute," Anna said softly to Aunt Maria. "By themselves."

"Oh, Anna!" Aunt Maria exclaimed. "They do look like that. I'm glad you pointed it out to me. There were such lovely parties years ago. That's why I think these are historical slippers."

"If you're really going to keep them, Maria," Aunt Eleanor said, "please get them out of here. I've got enough to keep track of."

Aunt Maria and Anna carried the slippers back to the kitchen—armfuls of slippers that could dance by themselves.

Anna brought a grocery bag for the slippers. On its side, Aunt Maria carefully wrote, with a leftover black crayon: Historical Society. Anna put the historical bag behind the big flour can on the pantry floor.

Next time, in Grandmother's room, nobody said *slipper* or *gown* or *historical*.

Aunt Maria said, "Here we are."

Anna said, "This is the last possible box for now."

Priscilla said, "Am I ever tired!"

Aunt Eleanor said, "I know they sell rags by the pound at the charities. So this will be a box of old nightgowns and old towels, and things like that. And Grandmother's sheets, all of those old sheets." She took a funny breath and frowned at Aunt Maria.

Aunt Maria looked puzzled. "Are Mother's sheets that thin, Eleanor?" she asked.

"That thin," said Aunt Eleanor abruptly. She turned from Aunt Maria. "Priscilla, it's time for more boxes."

"Hurry up, Anna," said Priscilla. "My mother needs boxes."

When they brought Aunt Eleanor three more boxes, she said, "You better get more right away. In case it starts to snow. You can't be on those stairs in the snow."

"Not again!" Priscilla complained.

On this trip down to the basement, Anna led the way.

"Those dumb sheets take too much room. They aren't thin at all," Priscilla suddenly said from behind Anna. She said it as though Anna had been arguing with her and was about to lose. "My mother has to tell Aunt Maria that they are, and make her believe it. Otherwise, she'd keep them forever and never use them. And sit there and cry over a bunch of sheets."

Anna didn't expect to reply, but the words rushed out. "They probably are thin."

"I know they're not. My mother told my father the whole thing last night."

"You shouldn't make fun of it when somebody cares because her mother died."

"Aunt Maria never knows what to do."

"She's doing things now."

"She is not. My mother's doing it all."

"But it's Aunt Maria whose mother died. Grandmother was important. You don't know anybody else who had dancing slippers like that, for parties."

"Anna, you're such a goof!" Priscilla was mad now. "You don't understand anything about Aunt Maria! Give me the basement keys. I'm going down by myself. Get out of the way!"

Anna listened to Priscilla, slapping downward.

You get hot when you're mad, she thought shakily, *but afterward you're colder than ever.*

She climbed back up to the apartment. She opened the kitchen door with as little noise as possible. In the few minutes during which she had been fighting with Priscilla on the back stairs, the kitchen had changed. Something loud and awful was happening at a distance in the apartment. It seemed to Anna that the whole kitchen was straining and listening to it.

She held the door handle as though it would keep her from sinking. She pushed the door toward closing, to keep out as much of the cold as she could without allowing a telltale click.

Aunt Eleanor was screaming. "It's absolutely ridiculous! You never go anyplace! You don't even like jewelry! What do you want with her rings?"

"They're mine. I don't care if I never go anyplace."

"Maria, for God's sake, don't be insane. It isn't safe for an old maid living alone here to have diamonds like that."

"I'm perfectly safe in my own house."

"There! What did I tell you? That's just what I'm trying to say. Wouldn't you look silly wearing diamond rings in here? You never get dressed up."

Aunt Maria was not crying. She said, maybe shakily but bravely for her, "Mother gave them to me."

"MAYBE THAT'S WRONG!"

After that scream, there was silence for a minute. Anna felt as though she were pasted against the silence.

She's never this mean. Aunt Eleanor never screams. Nobody screams like that. Poor Aunt Maria!

When Aunt Eleanor started again, she wasn't screaming. But her plain loudness had a mean sound of its own. "We'll see what Charles has to say. Don't be surprised, Maria, if he says that valuable rings must be taken care of—for the future."

There was an oversized thump. Anna recognized the sound. One of them had slammed down the seat of the hall tree.

"Even putting them in here." Aunt Eleanor's voice was staying loud. "This is no hiding place for valuable rings. And in a rubber galosh. What if I had packed that for the charities? I almost did. If you hadn't shown up accidentally and remembered."

"Not accidentally," Aunt Maria responded with dignity.

Anna smiled. She cheered for Aunt Maria by tightening and loosening her hold on the doorknob.

"Stop," Aunt Eleanor demanded. "Stop all of this, Maria. The girls will be back up in a few minutes. I'm not going to go into this anymore, in front of them."

Anna eased the door open and stepped out onto the cold landing again. As soon as she heard Priscilla, she started down to meet her.

Priscilla had a load of folded-down boxes. She was bringing up three of them, all by herself. She was struggling with them. She was looking messy and mad.

"I'll take a couple," Anna offered.

"Why can't you take them all?"

This time, it was quiet in the apartment, near and far. Priscilla threw her coat on a chair and marched out of the kitchen.

Once again, Aunt Maria and Anna were box pasters. Aunt Maria's eyes weren't red. But Anna felt safer looking down. Aunt Maria's hands, as they once again ironed paper tape, looked like nice ordinary old hands.

They would be just right for old-fashioned rings.

"You're a help, Anna dear. I'm glad you came."

Five

Through the next part of the day, Aunt Eleanor and Aunt Maria didn't meet once, anywhere in the apartment.

At two o'clock exactly, Aunt Maria said to Anna, "It's so late! You must all be starved. I have some chicken soup. I think everyone would like that, don't you, Anna? With some sandwiches. And there are always cookies."

Anna had just finished bringing the contents of Grandmother's medicine cabinet to Aunt Maria in the kitchen. Aunt Maria, with curiosity and patience, had lined the bottles and jars and tubes and drugstore cylinders in short, neat rows on the kitchen table. She had looked at each one before she dropped it into the wastebasket.

Saying good-bye. Not blaming any of you because Grandmother died.

At lunch, Aunt Maria and Aunt Eleanor didn't look at each other. Priscilla didn't notice anything.

She was talking about the basement.

"I should think you'd be afraid to go down there alone, Aunt Maria. It's horrible!"

"I don't want you down there alone, Priscilla," Aunt Eleanor declared.

With a little frown, Priscilla looked at Anna, then looked away. She meant: I *was* down there alone and it's all your fault.

Aunt Maria said, "We used to have three custodians. They tended to everything for us, including all the lockers. I remember them. . . . " Her voice trailed away.

"It's quite hard for Charles to find even a good part-time janitor for you nowadays."

"But the work is lighter. They don't have to shovel coal."

"There's other work, Maria. A janitor now should be capable of—for instance—keeping records for Charles. It's not like years ago."

The delicate sound of soup spoons clinking continued for a while after that. Spoon talked to spoon. None of the people talked much through all the rest of lunch.

"Very good lunch, Maria," Aunt Eleanor finally said. "Don't bother about dinner. I'll take the girls to Marty's Most, for a bite. That's all we'll want, with this big lunch being so late. You and Charles can talk about whatever you have to, while we're gone." She stood up. "I'll need both you girls with me now," she said.

Aunt Maria would be alone in the kitchen, with

the wonderful soup smell and the quiet spoons and the dishwater. Anna wished she could stay with her.

✦   ✦   ✦

It was nearly dusk, with all the lights turned on in Grandmother's bedroom, when Aunt Maria came into the room. Aunt Eleanor had just finished filling a box. She was standing next to it, at the side of Grandmother's bed. Anna and Priscilla were sitting back to back on the sides of the chaise longue. They were leaning against each other.

"Boy, did we do a bunch of stuff!" Priscilla said.

"It was like chasing a lot of kittens around, Aunt Maria," Anna said.

"They scoot fast, I know, Anna. You have to hurry. From place to place. We have so many drawers in here."

"Yes," said Aunt Eleanor. "I'm glad you realize that, Maria. I for one have got to sit down. I'll do it now. I have some calls to make, in any case."

They heard her walk down the hall. The door of Aunt Maria's bedroom, where the telephone was, shut behind Aunt Eleanor.

Aunt Maria said, "I'll get the three formal dresses down now. The ones that go with their own dancing slippers." She looked up to the closet shelves as though they were full of moonlight.

"That's what those three big boxes are," she continued, in the moonlight. "On the top shelf."

Anna brought the step stool from the kitchen for Aunt Maria. She stood next to her and reached up for the first dusty box that Aunt Maria was lifting down.

"I get the next one, Anna," Priscilla said. "Don't open yours yet. I want to see."

While Priscilla was carrying the second box to the oilcloth-covered bed, Anna took the third box.

"Good!" said Aunt Maria, in general joy. She helped Anna bring the third box to the bed.

Box carriers. Experienced. We do the job right. Anna smiled.

Priscilla said, "Ugh! The dust!"

The third box was the only one that was paper wrapped. Aunt Maria looked at all the boxes happily. Then she started to unfold that wrapping paper. "I feel like opening this one first."

The box was so old, it seemed as though it had turned into blotting paper, dull gray and grainy. Anna helped Aunt Maria ease the top off. Aunt Maria took the dress out. She held it up for the girls to see.

The dress was floor-length: sheer black wool with long sleeves. It had a stiff standing black collar, like the Sisters' white ones. Two rows of small jet buttons started at the collar line and went down the front of the dress to the hem. Above the hem, circling the bottom of the dress, around and around, were many close rows of black ribbon braid.

There was a piece of thick, folded, ivory-colored writing paper left in the bottom of the box.

"See what it is, Anna." Aunt Maria was peeking around the dress.

Anna unfolded it. Six more of the jet buttons were neatly sewn to the paper. Under the buttons was written, so carefully that the letters looked like a collection of small drawings: *Funeral. The Honorable Arthur McCanon. Mayor. Friday, November 27, 1874.*

"Some party!" Priscilla said.

"This isn't a party dress, dear," Aunt Maria said earnestly. She was holding the dress aside her body now, and looking around at it.

"I do exactly remember this dress. I was just a little girl. But I remember. Charles wouldn't. He was too little. My mother used to show this dress sometimes. If someone wondered about the dress. That's what I remember."

"*Who* wondered?" Priscilla asked.

Aunt Maria said, "I think the President came . . . "

"Hoh!" Priscilla interrupted.

Aunt Maria finished, ". . . to the funeral." And added, "I am delighted by the extra buttons."

"Well, I sure hope something better is in the other boxes," said Priscilla.

The next dress was lime green.

"This is a pretty one," said Aunt Maria.

Moonlight . . . moonlight . . . summer garden . . . thought Anna.

"It's wonderful," said Aunt Maria. Before she took it out of the box, she asked Anna to get the matching slippers. Anna brought the historical grocery bag.

Aunt Maria set the lime-green slippers as precisely as standing feet on the polished floor. ("Such a small size!") Placing herself behind the slippers, she held the dress up closely against her body.

"You see how Mother looked? That was a nice party, don't you think? You girls would have liked it."

Anna would have loved it. The sleeves of the party dress won her heart immediately. From the shoulders, they flowed in a prodigal spending of gossamer cloth down to thick cuffs made out of polished ribbon. The same gossamer green was a frosting on the whole dress underneath, which, Anna was sure, would rustle with every princess step.

She asked, "Aunt Maria, what was the party?"

"I'll try to remember for you, Anna," Aunt Maria answered and, without pondering, went on. "A party in the summer. Lanterns in the garden. A wedding reception!" she exclaimed. "Yes, it must have been a wedding reception. Mother went to a lot of receptions. But I'm thinking that she wore this dress many special times."

"Sure," said Priscilla.

She was opening the third box.

The third dress had been folded and boxed for years. Anna had no trouble believing that. She had trouble for a minute believing that she was still Anna.

I am standing here. This is me, at Aunt Maria's apartment.

The third dress was yellow. The startling thing about the yellow dress—the thing that made Anna unbelievable to Anna for that weird minute— slipped out of the box first, before the dress was even unfolded. It was the misty identity of the dress.

Anna thought that she couldn't breathe right. *This is a princess dress of mine.* Anna stared. *So much alike. I never thought that someone I . . . I knew would really have one.*

Priscilla brought the yellow matching slippers.

Aunt Maria held this gown up, too—above the slippers that belonged to it. Anna touched the real yellow dress. She touched the wide sash. The skirt was as she had designed it: a gigantic upside-down flower, a tulip in shape.

"You favor this one, Anna." Aunt Maria was delighted. "I can tell that you do."

Anna said, barely out loud, "It looks like a princess dress in a fairy tale."

Aunt Maria responded, "Of course it does."

"What do we do with them now?" Priscilla asked.

Aunt Maria answered happily, "Let's put them in the spare bedroom. The dresses and the bag of slippers. Everything will be together. I am certain that the historical society will be interested. Especially in the Mayor's dress."

"The Mayor's dress. That's funny," Priscilla said.

Anna was breathing ordinarily again. "Should we leave the dresses unfolded on the spare beds, Aunt Maria?" she asked.

Aunt Maria beamed. "They could breathe that way!"

Anna carried the old dresses, one by one. They felt only like old dresses in her arms. An old black dress, an old green dress. An old yellow dress.

Priscilla left the bag of slippers for Aunt Maria to carry; she didn't go near the spare bedroom. Anna and Aunt Maria lingered there, looking at the dresses spread out.

Aunt Maria said, "We better go, to see if Eleanor needs us. You're like me, Anna. Old things are so nice."

Six

When Uncle Charles returned, it was Anna who went to open the door for him. She tried to wish that Uncle Charles would tell Aunt Eleanor (just the two of them talking, but as soon as possible), "That stuff about the diamond rings is silly. Let Maria have them."

What he said—over Anna's head, to Aunt Eleanor—was, "I didn't get a chance to call you back about—"

"We've had a long day, Charles," Aunt Eleanor interrupted quickly.

"Call you back about the diamond rings." Anna was sure. *Aunt Eleanor means, "You better not talk about the diamonds now—because the girls will hear."*

"I'm going to take Priscilla and Anna to Marty's Most for hamburgers," Aunt Eleanor was going on. "You and Maria will get a chance to talk about everything, while we're gone. I'm sure she'll be able to find something for dinner for you."

"The wake is tomorrow night. The funeral is Thursday," Uncle Charles said. "The day before Christmas. It's the only funeral that day. We had our choice of times. Nine o'clock's best for the Mass. I don't know anybody outside family who'll come. None of their friends are left." Then he repeated, "The day before Christmas."

"The children's party should be that night," Aunt Eleanor said. "Poor Priscilla. And Anna. And Michael. Everyone always enjoys that party, Charles. It's a shame."

It's certainly mean of Grandmother to have her funeral on Christmas Eve Day.

✦   ✦   ✦

When Anna and Priscilla and Aunt Eleanor stepped outside, they formed an instant, automatic huddle of three. The wind was stronger.

"Don't anybody talk. Save your breath, and hurry!" Aunt Eleanor ordered, breaking up the huddle.

Marty's Most was on the streetcar street, nearly the full block down from Aunt Maria's corner. It wasn't one of the places that could be seen from the living room's big windows.

When they were seated at a little table in Marty's, Aunt Eleanor said, "I feel like someone just threw wet sand in my face."

Marty's Most was full of steamy air and hamburger smells, crisscrossing from wall to wall.

"I like Marty's Most. Marty's Most Delicious!" Priscilla said, reciting the whole sign with enthusiasm.

"How many hamburgers?" Aunt Eleanor asked. "Two each?"

Aunt Eleanor had just a cup of coffee. "I don't object to these places," she said, while the girls were eating. "Marty's Most is all right for certain neighborhoods. It's too bad that this neighborhood has slipped so far. I'm sure Grandmother never even knew that this was here, a block away."

"I wonder what was here. When Grandmother was young." Anna looked around the steamy, white-walled restaurant. The restaurant itself was not worth wondering about—as everyday as an ice box. "What was here, I wonder. When Grandmother was wearing her party dresses."

"That Mayor's dress is some party dress!" Priscilla talked on about the dresses, mostly making fun of the Mayor's dress.

Poor old Priscilla. She had a chance to like the dresses. She likes Marty's Most better.

When Priscilla finally finished, Aunt Eleanor said, "I've been wondering if Grandmother didn't just forget to get rid of them. Of all people to find them first, it would have to be Maria. She does too much of that living in the past. It isn't healthy. Not good for the mind."

The girls chewed. Aunt Eleanor sipped. Marty's Most steamed.

When they were ready to leave, Priscilla said, "Old Marty's Most makes you really warmer. It could last a while, if we could just run."

"You can't," Aunt Eleanor declared. "Don't get out of my sight."

They walked as fast as they could, Aunt Eleanor huddling into her white coat.

Inside the apartment building, Aunt Eleanor was first up the stairs, Anna last. Uncle Charles opened the apartment door. Anna heard him before she saw him.

"Maria's in the living room."

"I know," Aunt Eleanor answered carelessly.

They didn't take off their coats.

Aunt Maria was sitting on the velvet sofa that stood against the long wall in the living room.

"Oh. You're rag knitting," Aunt Eleanor remarked.

In a sizeable heap on the sofa next to Aunt Maria was her knitting material—lengths of rag-bag cloth and some dyed cotton stocking pieces all sewn together to make hugely overgrown yarn, which Aunt Maria would turn into thick, soft rugs. Anna hesitated for a minute, then walked over to the sofa. She sat down near the knitting rags.

Priscilla crossed the room to the big chair. She sat down. Her parents stood. They were not close together, but Uncle Charles appeared particularly bony in a room with Aunt Eleanor's big white winter coat.

Aunt Maria's knitting needles could have been posts for a small fence. Anna was used to them, and to the rag yarn. She wasn't used to the feeling now—that she should say something good about rag knitting.

The new rug was mostly apple red and bright green. "This is going to be finished for Christmas, Anna," said Aunt Maria. "It has to be. With all this red and green."

Aunt Maria did not look as though she had been crying about any diamonds that might be taken away from her soon.

"I hope everything is settled," Aunt Eleanor said.

Aunt Maria raised her head from her knitting. "I don't like wakes. Priscilla shouldn't go to the wake," she said.

"Maria settled one thing," contributed Uncle Charles. "No. She doesn't want anybody to stay with her tonight. There's nothing else we can do now. The sooner we go, the better."

"Priscilla shouldn't go to the wake," Aunt Maria repeated pleasantly.

"Of course not," Aunt Eleanor said, and frowned. "She'll be with Anna, right after school. Until we all get home from the wake."

"The wake lasts until nine tomorrow night, even if nobody comes," said Uncle Charles. "That's late for Priscilla and Anna to be at the Halders' alone."

"Charles, it's safe," Aunt Maria said. "And it will be enjoyable with little Michael there, too." She smiled at Anna. "You'll all be enjoying each other," she said.

Enjoying isn't the right word for this discussion about wake night. Anna was staring down at the rag yarn and waiting for Aunt Eleanor to say so.

But Aunt Eleanor said nothing.

Uncle Charles, however, said something. "It's time for us to go," he said.

At the door of the apartment, Aunt Maria told Priscilla, "Don't you worry about the wake. Have a good time with Anna. That's better."

"Yes," said Priscilla.

Anna said, "I love my rag rug, Aunt Maria—the one you made for me last year."

Aunt Maria was pleased. "I don't remember what color it is."

"Brown mostly, with pink and yellow."

"I could teach you how to knit rugs, Anna. It's the easiest kind of knitting. I learned in Michigan. In the dunes."

"Settle it later," Uncle Charles said.

"What do the dunes have to do with it?" Priscilla asked.

"That would be a long story," Aunt Eleanor replied. "We've got to leave. Maria, we'll be back tomorrow. You know that. You might work on a list tonight. Something like Charles' list. Things to do."

"I might," said Aunt Maria.

This time, on the return Schwannmobile ride, Aunt Eleanor talked a lot.

"We did a good job with Grandmother's old things today, Charles. The girls were a marvelous help. So much should have been thrown out years ago."

Uncle Charles didn't comment. Aunt Eleanor didn't need him to. "I did get a chance to make those other calls, Charles. I told you about them on the phone. Not only Eileen Densch, although she was the important one, because she could have stayed tonight with Maria if Maria wanted her to. I called the Schores. And Ted said . . . "

There was more after that. Anna didn't hear it. Now, in the smooth Schwannmobile, rough worries tried to come back—about the cold kitchen and the screaming. So Anna was thinking hard— about the three custodians, years ago. She was wondering if they wore uniforms. *With brass buttons? No, because they shoveled coal.*

Priscilla grabbed Anna's arm. She pulled close, put her lips almost on Anna's hat, and hissed, "I forgot the keys! I don't know where the keys are!"

Aunt Eleanor half turned just then and started talking to the backseat. Anna stared hopelessly at the side of Aunt Eleanor's face. Shadows flashed across it as The Schwannmobile passed streetlights.

"I hope you didn't miss too much schoolwork today, Anna. Tell your teacher you were a real help. Are you having a Christmas party there? I suppose you are. Anna, enjoy it. I'd feel terrible if all this about Grandmother spoiled your Christmas party."

She turned back and started telling Uncle Charles now about all the things that Anna and Priscilla did. That took a long time—while The Schwannmobile went on and on, farther and farther from the lost basement keys and the possibility of finding them safe.

After miles and miles, Aunt Eleanor turned again, held her hand out over the back of the front seat, and said, "Now I'll just take the keys back, Anna."

"I don't have the keys, Aunt Eleanor."

Priscilla yelled, "I bet they're in the basement door!"

"Anna! Look in your pocket," ordered Aunt Eleanor. "Are you sure you don't have the keys?"

"I don't have them. Aunt Eleanor, I'm sorry."

"Charles, we have to go back!"

It wasn't easy to go back. The lake drive was a continuous road without exits until The Schwannmobile got a long way past the Pier. It didn't look lovely to Anna now, on the way back. She couldn't think about anything safe. She had to think about lost keys in a basement door in Aunt Maria's bad neighborhood.

Uncle Charles parked The Schwannmobile in front of the apartment building. He didn't park smoothly; the grand automobile jerked.

Uncle Charles pulled out the keys. "Keep these, and lock my door," he said to Aunt Eleanor. "I'm going around the side of the building. Damn! Anyone could have gone that way, anytime they wanted."

He left the car. They watched him disappear.

Anna felt like a starched rag. *Anyone, anytime they wanted.*

"We're not even sure the keys are there, in the door." Aunt Eleanor's voice was cold. "They could be on the back stairs. Or fallen off the stairs. We'd have to search in daylight."

"I'm scared!" wailed Priscilla.

"And you're just as much to blame as Anna is," Aunt Eleanor said sharply.

They saw Uncle Charles stride around the corner of the building. Aunt Eleanor unlocked the door for him. Uncle Charles threw the ring of basement keys onto the front seat before he got in.

"You got them! Good!" exclaimed Aunt Eleanor.

"No, it's not good. The outside door was wide open, waiting for the next one who wanted to walk in. The keys were on the floor, inside the locker."

"Daddy! Are you going to call the police?"

"Charles, what did they take? Can you tell? What would anybody want? Why would they . . . "

"They didn't take anything," Uncle Charles interrupted, starting the car. "I don't care about that. They could have the whole locker and everything in it, and I wouldn't miss it. But I'm not going to let anyone get the idea that the building is here for the picking. I'll have the locks changed. Tomorrow!"

"One more thing, on such a bad day!" Aunt Eleanor complained.

There was nothing more to say. The Schwannmobile—with everyone inside it keeping the silence—started and moved and glided, and properly turned again onto the lake drive.

Anna was feeling that the big ring of keys on the front seat was white-hot and glowing, with all the miserableness and the lies it contained.

Aunt Eleanor broke into the silence. "Anna, forget about the keys. Don't feel bad at all. Don't even tell your mother. It's just part of the terrible confusion. You saw that. I should have checked on the keys. But there are always a thousand things a person could check on, in that place."

"I *am* sorry, Aunt Eleanor."

"Mother said to forget it. She just said that!"

"Priscilla's right. Just have a good Christmas party, Anna, in spite of everything."

Anna thought she saw Uncle Charles' shoulders tighten. Under the plaid blanket, she sank lower on the rich backseat of The Schwannmobile.

"What about our party, Mother?" Priscilla

asked. "Can't we have our party? It won't seem like Christmas. You always have the party for us."

"We should," said Aunt Eleanor. "We really should. We've had the children's party every year since the girls were babies. It would be a shame to break off. Charles?"

"Not now. About the party," said Uncle Charles.

It was settled then with the Schwanns. They wouldn't be mentioning the Christmas party again.

Anna suddenly missed the party very much. She was relieved that there would be no more connecting the lost party with Grandmother's inconvenient dying. But she did know now that Aunt Eleanor was right about breaking off. Breaking off the party that belonged on Christmas Eve would leave an empty space in everyone's life. A space without the lights and the carols that were supposed to be there.

Seven

Anna said good night to Aunt Eleanor and Priscilla before anybody got out of the car. She knew that they were as glad as she was that the deep cold made more than saying good-bye impossible.

Uncle Charles escorted Anna across Hunt Street as usual, no talking along the way. Uncle Charles rang the doorbell. Said, "I won't come in," to Anna's mother. Turned, and left.

"Good night, Charles," Anna's mother called after him.

She closed the big front door. She asked, "How are you, Anna?"

"Awful."

The German chime clock was striking—striking far too slowly—as Anna walked past her mother. All the notes, those that announced the hour and those that followed and counted the hour—eight o'clock now—were painfully draggy.

"Daddy forgets to wind the clock!" Anna turned

back quickly and hugged her mother.

"You can't tell him now, Anna," her mother said softly, in the vicinity of Anna's hair. "Daddy's in bed already. And he hasn't been home twenty minutes yet. He said he felt as though he's been completely absorbed with this—all the time since yesterday, all the time since Aunt Rose died, and needing to catch his breath now. I wonder if you do that while you sleep—catch your breath?" She waited a minute. Anna didn't comment about breath catching. "Anna," her mother then asked, "why would the clock make you so miserable?"

Not the clock. It's just wrong, too.

"Priscilla is such a dope," Anna told her mother's shoulder. "And everyone's mean to Aunt Maria."

"I know what you're thinking, about Aunt Maria, Anna. But they're not really mean to her. Remember—we were saying that Uncle Charles ought to listen to himself? It sometimes might sound mean. You hear it that way. But I don't think Maria does. You haven't seen her get upset, have you?"

"I didn't see her. But I heard her. She was awfully upset, Mother."

Anna's mother stepped back. She said, "Oh, I'm so sorry!"

Anna went on, in a rush, "It was about Grandmother's diamond rings. Aunt Maria has them now. Grandmother gave them to her. Aunt Eleanor doesn't think . . . she doesn't think that

Aunt Maria is smart enough to take care of them. She yelled at Aunt Maria."

"Anna, why on earth did she do that in front of you? And Priscilla!"

"Not Priscilla," Anna answered. "Priscilla was in the basement."

Anna told her mother about standing alone in the kitchen and hearing the distant fight. When she finished, her mother said, "Poor Maria. I wish it hadn't happened." She paused, looked briefly over Anna's head, then back to Anna's face. "It's probably hard, Anna, for anyone to be calm about diamonds."

"Aunt Eleanor didn't even try to be calm."

Her mother held up her hand, like a gentle stop sign.

"Everything wasn't bad today, was it?" she asked.

Priscilla was. But that's baby tattling.

"No, everything wasn't," Anna said.

"Tell me," her mother requested. "Anna dear, tell me something good."

"Something was good," Anna said. "We found some of Grandmother's old dresses."

She told her mother about the black dress— what it looked like—and its history written on old heavy paper, with beautiful buttons sewn onto the paper and onto the history.

"Aunt Rose," her mother murmured. "I'll bet people had to be invited to a mayor's funeral in those days."

Anna went on to describe the green dress with its green matching slippers.

Her mother said, "I have such a lovely picture in my mind—of Aunt Rose in those dresses."

But not Aunt Rose in the yellow dress. I won't tell about that. It's too close to Johnny talk.

"Of course," Anna said, "Priscilla acted bored with the dresses."

"You could forget about Priscilla right away, if you wanted to," her mother said. "You have homework. Leo McVene brought it after school. I put his letter on your desk."

Priscilla evaporated then and there. Anna felt pleasantly warm.

"I better go see what Sister Elizabeth thinks I can do tonight." Halfway up the stairs, Anna turned back. Her mother was still standing in the hall.

"I love you," Anna said.

Her mother said, "Oh, Anna, I love you, too."

✦   ✦   ✦

There were two sheets of paper in the envelope on Anna's desk. The first was a note from Sister Elizabeth.

Is sloppy writing a sin? Sisters are so super neat.

My dear Anna,

Please accept the Sisters' sympathy and promise

of prayer at the death of your relative. Your mother told me about your generosity in helping at this sad time. I am well aware that you knew death more closely just a short time ago.

Anna's hand was shaking the beautiful penmanship.

How could Johnny have been such a nice little baby, then turn into something spooky?

Anna didn't finish reading the neat letter. For the time being, she dropped it into her wastebasket.

She tipped her desk chair back, and stared at her rag-knitted rug. She began to wander into thinking about holding Aunt Maria's big knitting needles herself. She imagined Anna Halder, knitting perfectly, and a beautiful Christmas-colored rug getting bigger and bigger.

Anna's chin relaxed. It had to, because she was smiling.

She lowered her chair. She unfolded the second sheet of writing paper. Sister Elizabeth's model penmanship was also on the second sheet, at the top. Anna approached it with caution, but the whole thing was only about the homework.

Anna,

Without knowing of your situation, I was thinking of you last night when I wrote out today's assignment. It was in the back of my mind that

Anna Halder will enjoy this, if anyone can enjoy homework. Leo McVene generously volunteered to copy the assignment here for you, and deliver it and my note to your house on the way home.

Sister Elizabeth

Leo's writing, following Sister's, was pretty neat itself. It was a lot bigger all around than Sister Elizabeth's.

The assignment was called "A Christmas List."

Select three people, real or imaginary, living or historical, humble or famous. Describe the Christmas gift you would choose for each se-lected person this year, and explain your choice. Examples: a family member, Queen Victoria, President Roosevelt, the Pope, Hiawatha, Vir-ginia Dare, or anyone you encounter in daily living. You may make up a character, if you wish. Use your good imagination.

Leo had added a message, down at the bottom of the page:

Sister said if you didn't have time to write the list, OK.

Sincerely, Leo McVene

P.S. Sledding was great at Clark Hill. George Farley thought he broke his leg. But he didn't.

LMcV

Anna carefully tore Leo's note off the sheet. She tore against the metal edge of her ruler,—a process Sister Elizabeth encouraged, to rescue the last bits of usable school paper. Anna folded the note. It was small, unnoticeable. She put it under the pencil box in her drawer.

Anna picked up a pencil. She rubbed the pencil up and down with the tip of her index finger—but for just a little while. It didn't take Anna long to accept a name that had been creeping into her thoughts. Leo McVene. Anna didn't write even the initials.

She started to do the homework. She wrote on scrap paper.

1. Person: An imaginary seventh grader at Mercy Grammar. Gift: A house with a library. Reason: This person loves to read, and I would want to give a perfect place for reading. My gift library is large. Many polished brown-wood bookcases are really full of books, not of such things as knickknacks, or picture frames, or vases. There is a fireplace, a particularly comfortable thing as part of a December gift. I would give a snowstorm at Christmastime, too, if I could.

Anna rubbed her hand over the writing as though it were a smooth possession.

Sister Elizabeth will love this.

Anna Halder, enjoying homework, was instantly certain about Person Two. Aunt Maria.

2. Person: An old lady I know. Gift: A special exhibit at the historical society. Reason: This lady hopes that the historical society will want some beautiful old clothing that belonged to her mother. In the special gift exhibit (which the historical society is very glad to have), she would get a chance to see her mother's party dresses and slippers worn by mannequins. There would be elegant old wooden furniture and Oriental rugs and gas lamps as background. The exhibit would open at Christmastime and then become permanent.

Anna was satisfied. She felt that she was grinning like the Cheshire Cat in the tree. *But much kinder, and completely sensible.*

Aunt Maria would be satisfied, too, if she ever knew. She would be more than satisfied—Aunt Maria would be blissful.

Anna kept thinking about Aunt Maria, enjoying this Christmas present. Then Anna's mind was taking the ride home from Aunt Maria's apartment, on a peaceful dark winter night, in The Schwann-mobile.

"I know Number Three," Anna whispered.

3. Person: The downtown Pier. Gift: All new

white paint. Reason: The new paint is important. The Pier is beautiful at night, with all the bright lights that are around it. But the Pier is raggedy-looking in the daylight because you can see that its paint is peeling off. If it were painted pure white again, it would be beautiful at all times, at night with the lights, and during the day with sunshine on the pure-white Pier and on the waters close by.

Anna wanted to say something more—about getting the Pier ready for Christmas. But the thought stayed mushy. She couldn't make it firm.

"I'm as tired as Daddy," she said out loud.

She looked at her scrap paper. There seemed to be an impossibly wide puddle of scrap paper. All she could do now was gather the paper, to make the puddle smaller.

She started down the stairs just as her mother started up. Anna waited for her.

"I'm glad you're right here, Mother. I think I'm too tired to go halfway down, even. I'll set my alarm. But would you please be sure to wake me up twenty minutes early, if I don't hear the alarm? I did my homework, but I haven't copied it yet."

Anna was sure that she went to sleep instantly. She was also sure that she made a short, remarkable speech when the seventh-grade class forgot itself and clapped for her amazingly interesting, colorful Christmas list.

Eight

With Christmas so near, the school tree was lighted all day, not just at dismissal time. It stood like a mass of happiness near the front door of the building. The seventh grade had just been there, to take their class turn at singing carols.

Christmas was flooding in under the doors and through the windows, and getting everybody a little bit silly. Sister Elizabeth regularly had to say, "Settle down, people. Please!"

Now, after the carols, Sister was ordering, "People, don't sing anymore. We've finished carol singing for the moment."

She measured the silliness in the air. "All right. We'll skip spelling and English grammar. We'll go right on and read some of our Christmas lists."

Jane Carney volunteered. Her list was short and dull. Anna was embarrassed for her.

Steven Fariotis was next. At the end, he read,

"For Sister Elizabeth. Present: The Fariotis promise to study diagramming sentences. Reason: Because Sister would like Fariotis to be as good at it as she is."

"Would I, Steven? For a Christmas present?" Sister asked evenly.

Someone started by yelling, "Sure!" Others joined in.

Sister stared them down. She waited a silent minute, then asked, "Anna, did you have time to do the homework?"

Anna started to read her Christmas list. As she read, the list kept sounding good to Anna.

Writing, Anna was sure, was like placing the pieces of the miniature village, but the pieces were words and ideas. Each piece was neat and precise—and waiting to become different in surprising ways when you moved it and felt it settle.

Anna could tell whenever she read out a good part of her Christmas list, because it felt so great.

She finished. She knew instantly that she was the only person in the room who felt great about anything on the list.

Right away, Martin Porter yelled—really exploded into yelling—from his desk at the back of the room, "Wow! Does she ever spend the money!"

Everybody started talking, commenting on that comment, not on any part of Anna's list.

Sister Elizabeth had to tap her desk bell: *bing,*

bing, bing, bing, bing. The bings finally got through. The noise died down.

Sister didn't scold with words. Into the silence of the seventh-grade room, Sister Elizabeth sighed. Just sighed. She hung her sigh on the silence and let it be shaming there.

Then she started a personal speech to Anna Halder.

"That's an interesting list, Anna. Imaginative, and correct and well-written. As usual. I am sure that mature people"—here, Sister almost waved the hanging shame at all the other seventh graders— "would have responded to it appropriately."

She doesn't like it. Anna knew that positively, and almost heard the Christmas spirit drain away. Out under the door, out through all the window glass.

"Yes," said Sister Elizabeth slowly, making it a long, time-filling word. Then, she was brisk again. "Pass in your papers, please."

Sister watched Jane Carney bring the Christmas-list papers to her desk. Then, nicely, almost widely, totally unexpectedly, Sister Elizabeth smiled at the seventh grade.

"We'll clean desks now. For the new year. Each of you, talk to your desk." Sister smiled again. "*Whisper* to all the months of mess in there. Tell the mess it is leaving now. You will not need to talk to each other. From what you've just shown me, I know you'd disturb every other pupil in this building, if I allowed you so much as *one* word to *one* of your neighbors."

Most of the seventh grade smiled back.

"We'll need a wastebasket monitor," said Sister.

George Farley volunteered. Almost right away, he started to walk up and down the aisles, offering the big wastebasket for any trash that was ready.

Sister followed him, looking from desk to desk. Anna knew Sister wasn't really inspecting. Who would want to inspect all those blots and eraser crumbs? Sister was just—by her walking—making the seventh-grade Christmas spirit be still and behave. That spirit was like a balloon up high that might either break through the roof or pop, out loud, right in the room, if it weren't for Sister. Sister Elizabeth was balloon monitor.

When Sister got to Anna, she leaned down and said, very softly, "Please stay after school for a minute, Anna."

That softness was scary, and definite. Sister Elizabeth was going to tell Anna, in private, what was wrong with her Christmas list. *Something embarrassing.*

At dismissal time, Sister went out with the rest of the seventh grade. Anna knew that the others were walking very politely along the corridors and down the stairs, Sister Elizabeth still fearlessly monitoring that Christmas balloon.

Sister returned very soon. "Take a front desk, Anna. So we can talk."

Sister sat at her desk on the platform, looking down. Anna sat in Jane Carney's desk, looking up.

"Anna, you do write remarkably well for a seventh grader. Your imagination is a gift. It truly is."

"Thank you, Sister."

"I'm somewhat concerned about today, however."

Thank you, Sister. I'm somewhat concerned myself. Anna felt her tongue pressing some parts of those words against her teeth.

"It's nothing you did, Anna. It's something you didn't do."

With just a few more words from Sister, Anna understood that what she didn't do was: Be holy about Christmas. Sister said, "Anna, you didn't give Christ's holy peace on His own birthday to the close family of your relative who died."

Close family. That would be Aunt Maria. Aunt Maria already has that kind of peace. Aunt Maria needs peace of a littler kind, from maybe just one other Schwann. How could I give that to Aunt Maria? How could I possibly?

"Everything on your list was"—Sister hesitated, then found the correct guilty word—"material. Martin was correct. In his own loud way." Sister smiled down at Anna. "You did write only of gifts that involved a great deal of money." Sister thought that over. "A mansion. And an elaborate exhibition of clothes. Paint for the Pier. That's rather nice. But, again, costly. And material. Nothing on your list is in the holy spirit of Christmas. You see that, don't you, Anna?"

Anna nodded, remembering that—if you nod slowly—it looks polite.

Sister nodded back. They were silent for a long time. Anna wondered how to leave.

"Anna." Sister broke the silence with Anna's name spoken in her most delicate tone. "Might you not want to give your dear mother something meaningful this first Christmas since your baby brother died?"

Anna's first response came and went like a fright in a real bad dream at night: *My dear father! I have a dear father, too!*

She escaped from saying that. "Oh no, Sister!" she said instead. "Not in front of all the kids!"

That was almost sassing, almost out of bounds, but it increased Sister's patience and made her sad. "Anna, I may be wrong about your mother and the baby. Asking you to write about it now. It is still very tender. I begin to see. But I do think I should help you stretch your fine mind and discover deeper things to write about. Particularly at Christmas."

"Yessister."

"Yes," Sister agreed.

The talk was over, just in time. There was a knock at the classroom door. Leo McVene came in, carrying the seventh-grade wastebasket. "George left this at the incinerator."

"George would," Sister responded calmly. "Thank you, Leo."

While Anna was putting on her jacket, Sister talked about tomorrow's classroom party. Leo listened, waiting.

"Good-bye, children. Thank you for staying, Anna. God bless you both."

Anna and Leo walked without a word all the way down to the door of the building. Leo held the door for Anna.

"I guess we're still whispering to our desks," he said as they came out into the afternoon cold.

"It's like first grade," Anna said.

"I guess," Leo repeated.

Leo walked next to Anna. The sidewalk ahead looked to her as though it were going to stretch halfway around the world.

I can't think of one good thing to say. But I bet I could think of something great to say about my galoshes. Witty about galoshes, that's me.

Leo was studying his own galoshes. Looking downward, studying, Leo remarked, "I liked that library."

Anna sucked in her breath. "It's cold!" she exclaimed, recovering.

"Martin is sure one qualified yeller," Leo continued. He also continued watching his remarkable black galoshes, going forward on their own.

He said, to the galoshes, "I like the historical society. I go there, on the bus, whenever I want to."

The historical society, too.

"But," said Anna, "Sister Elizabeth didn't like anything."

"She didn't seem mad," Leo observed. "She's a pretty nice old nun."

"She wasn't mad. She was just being holy. She said my Christmas list was full of money. Not holy at all."

Leo looked up. Not at Anna. But up, straight ahead. Then, having seen what was straight ahead, Leo McVene exclaimed, "I'm really late!"

He started charging for the next corner. He turned it. He disappeared. Leo was gone before Anna could begin a single next word.

Priscilla Schwann was there, half a block straight ahead. Priscilla was running toward Anna. Then Priscilla was face to face, and puffing. Between puffs, she managed to talk. "Your mother said . . . I should come . . . to meet you. But I didn't know you . . . would be this far away. You've wasted so much time. Why didn't you . . . come home right away?"

"I was busy."

"We can go sledding . . . your mother said. I bet everyone's there already. Who was that boy?"

Anna answered, "A kid at school."

Priscilla had caught her breath. "Leo McVene. I know," she said. "Were you walking all the way with him? Do you always walk with him?"

"No. He's busy. He rescues wastebaskets."

"I don't care, Anna Halder. If you don't stop wasting time, and saying nutty things like that, we'll never get to Clark Hill."

"We'll get there," said Anna.

She walked her fastest. Priscilla kept up, after declaring, "I already ran this whole way once."

Nine

Clark Hill was a huge, deeply sloping vacant lot. It would have been three official city blocks wide if the downward dividing streets had ever been cut through. In the farthest corner of the hill, at the top, there was an extensive broken basement open to the sky. It was the foundation for an apartment building that had never been built. The basement was deep. Over the years, lots of people, winters and summers, had shifted chunks of concrete and big building stones and boards, and constructed a set of unreliable steps into the basement.

The foundation walls rose more than two feet above the ground, and were wide. People sat on the walls to rest, looking down into the basement at whoever had dared the steps and was down there, or looking out at sledders.

The deep, open foundation was ragged concrete. There were pieces of broken-off thick metal rope sticking out of the concrete walls in many places. The foundation was definitely a place for people to be very careful.

Anna had never seen Clark Hill so crowded. There were more adults than usual. Some of them were sledding with children who were too little to sled alone. Some were just enjoying sledding by themselves. And there seemed to be an awful lot of small-sized children sledding by themselves—sledding, and shouting and running and pushing on Clark Hill.

Anna and Priscilla climbed toward the foundation. Most of the starting mounds were in that area of the hill.

Out of a group at the center top of the hill—next in line—ran Leo McVene. He did a running bellyflop and gathered good speed.

Priscilla didn't notice. She had pulled ahead of Anna, and she stayed ahead, not looking back. Anna turned her head for one minute. She couldn't pick Leo McVene out of the crowd of sledders at the foot of the hill, at the end of that path.

Anna was always afraid that bellyflopping onto sledding snow would hurt more than summer bellyflopping onto water. She was even more afraid that she would start to run a sled bellyflop, then brake and stop in front of everybody, in obvious fear. She would be like a diver who almost jumps off the board but wilts, and can't do it—and maybe even cries.

There were always starting mounds on Clark Hill. They were as long and almost as wide as most sleds, shaped up like huge bricks, and curved down at the starting end. The first mounds got built each season. Anna was never there when they did. But like almost all the sledders on Clark Hill, Anna and Priscilla helped keep the mounds high enough and slick.

Laurette had loved to repair mounds. She did it better than anyone Anna had ever seen. Anna had once spent some time on Clark Hill, in a slow transparent snowfall, just standing and watching Laurette repair a mound. Laurette did it as though she had just heard someone moan, "That mound is awful! Nobody could get that mound right again!"

Watching Laurette repairing the mound (Laurette showing how silly a moan like that would be), Anna had imagined Laurette's mother sewing and saying dreamily, "But yes, little Laurette and little Anna. Take a snow and fix a mound."

Now Priscilla had one foot on a heavily rutted, gray mound. There were no sledders lined up waiting to use it.

"This one needs to be fixed," she said.

They carried new snow. They packed it on the sides. They jumped it down on the top.

"It's ready," Priscilla decided.

Drying off her mittens, rubbing the leather

palms up and down on the sides of her jacket, Anna looked at the new mound. "I like to repair mounds. They're better than snow forts. No one is going to waste time having a snowball war."

"I don't like snowball wars. At my school, some of the kids use ice balls."

"You can't do that at Mercy Grammar."

"So," said Priscilla, "send Sister Elizabeth over."

Anna grinned. "That's a good idea. She could melt the ice balls. One Elizabeth stare at one ice ball equals one cup of quick slush."

"Are you allowed," Priscilla asked seriously, "to call her Elizabeth?"

"No," said Anna. "You can go first."

It was a total joke. You have to start getting jokes, Priscilla. Or you'll be more and more like a lonesome old starting mound.

Priscilla sat upright on her sled. Anna gave her a strong starting push, in the middle of her back. By this time, there was a line of sledders forming behind Anna.

Priscilla yelled, "Gangway!"

It was Anna's turn. She lay down on her stomach on her sled. The sled was perched on the front curve of the mound. Anna inched up. She leaned out, as heavily forward as she could, and started propelling with her hands on the thin borders of the mound.

The person behind Anna helped now, with a great push on Anna's heels. Anna's sled tipped and moved and hit the path. In just the right way, it found the speedy tracks.

The packed-down snow of the path was super-fast. Anna felt like a champion sledder, magic on a magic hill. She was absolutely certain that this was the best ride she had ever had.

Anna's sled glided to a stop. She would have stayed there, relaxed now on her sled but still feeling the wonderful rush. But she knew the winter rules of Clark Hill. She got up immediately and pulled her sled out of the path, out of the way of the next sled coming down.

Priscilla hadn't waited at the bottom of the hill. Anna could see her, halfway back up again, tugging her sled.

"Hi."

Someone.

"If you want to bellyflop," Leo McVene said, "you have to run and crouch at the same time. Really crouch low. Otherwise, your sled digs in too deep and just stops."

"I don't like to bellyflop."

"You can't go really fast any other way. You like to go fast."

Anna was so surprised, she looked directly at Leo McVene. Leo McVene had just said to Anna Halder, on Clark Hill, "YOU like to go fast."

The winter afternoon was a shining icy shell, and Anna was warm inside it. Face to face, they spoke at the same time.

Leo: "Bellyflopping. Then you don't need the mounds."

Anna: "I've seen you, too."

"You should try it. Laurette did it sometimes. I used to see her." Leo hesitated, turned, and started running up the hill. He was carrying his sled.

Anna clomped up the hill, pulling hers. There were some words in Anna's head, wonderfully marking her climb, clomp by clomp by clomp.

I like . . . I like . . . I like . . . to go . . . fast . . . I like . . . I like . . .

"I saw you," Priscilla announced.

"So what?"

"So, Lovey-Dovey."

"If you want another push," Anna said, "we better get in line."

From then on, they sledded in pattern. Priscilla was always first, sitting up on her sled; Anna went second, flat on her sled, close to the snowy ground and watching it fly past her face.

Anna didn't know if she wanted to see Leo McVene on the hill again. She carefully didn't do any looking around whatsoever as she and Priscilla climbed back every time. It was still good sledding, but no longer the best sledding of Anna's life.

"Let's go sit on the foundation," Priscilla finally said. "I'm tired."

They sat together on the old wall, with their legs dangling into the dreary basement.

They didn't talk much. They just waved their legs a little, sometimes twisting their feet, galoshes and all.

Suddenly Priscilla yelled, "Hey! There's that dope again!" Almost directly opposite them, across the whole foundation, Leo McVene was climbing down the tumbled steps into the basement.

Across the whole foundation—that great empty echoing distance—Priscilla shouted again, louder this time. "She's over here!" She raised her arm high and arced her mitten down, pointing toward the middle of Anna's head. Leo looked up.

"I dare you to come over here!" Before Priscilla finished that shout, Anna had scrambled up. She grabbed for her sled rope, missed it, and grabbed again. The sled bounced a couple of times in turning. Then it followed fast as Anna pounded down Clark Hill, away from Priscilla.

There was a sudden series of high-pitched shrieks.

"NO! NO! NO!" Priscilla's voice.

Something like terror colored the shrieks. Anna stopped and jerked around. Priscilla was standing now, a couple of steps from her place at the edge of the foundation. Frozen in space, Priscilla was looking at two little kids. She didn't stop shrieking.

The little kids were half as tall as Priscilla. They were too small for Clark Hill at the dangerous edge of the basement foundation. A boy chasing a girl, they were running without looking, and would be crashing in an instant directly into Priscilla. From a distance, the scene looked unreal. Anna could not move. She just stared. She saw Priscilla hang her head and put her two big mittened hands across her face.

The little girl hit Priscilla.

Priscilla cried, "Ouch-o-o-w!"

When the boy plowed into the girl, Priscilla was thumped by both of them. She was fiercely pushed back. She sat down, hard against the uneven low wall of the foundation.

Priscilla yelled. She started to cry. In a second, she was sobbing gigantically. Now Anna could move. She tried to get back up the hill, dragging her sled, but she couldn't do it fast.

There was a crowd around Anna—people of all sizes hurrying to the accident. Someone running up kicked Anna's sled. Leo McVene was there suddenly.

The two little children were crying, loud and fast enough to be heard, even next to Priscilla's screaming.

Suddenly, Anna could see that there was blood on the little boy's face, running, with a startling redness, from his nose. Some of it got into his mouth. He coughed and spat.

Anna's stomach turned. She frowned her eyes shut, and she shuddered.

"It's only a nosebleed," Leo said.

There were no city guards on Clark Hill, the

way there were summer lifeguards on the beaches. The city probably didn't even know about Clark Hill and winter sledding there. But someone did take over—a man about as old as Anna's father, younger than Uncle Charles.

"You're being foolish," the man said loudly, helping Priscilla stand up. "You're not hurt that much. And nobody fell in. You'd feel better if you would . . ."

Standing up gave Priscilla's screams room to be bigger. The man shook her by the shoulders. ". . . if you would stop yelling." He took his hands away, stepped back, and watched Priscilla.

She saw Anna, and reached out toward her. "Anna!" sobbed Priscilla.

"You her sister?" the man asked quickly.

"I'll go and get her mother," Leo volunteered.

"Just a minute, son. We don't need a screaming mother, too," the man said. He turned to Priscilla. "Walk," he ordered. "Let me see you walk."

Stiffly, her arms hanging and not moving back and forth, Priscilla walked. Anna thought that the very short walk looked like pain in motion. Priscilla was sniffling and gulping.

"You're okay," the man decided. "You're just scared. Have your sister"—he noticed Leo—"and your friend walk you home. Take it easy."

The man turned back to the two little kids. He pushed his way through the crowd that was around them now. For a minute, Anna could see the little boy, with red blood staining through the handkerchief on his face.

"Anna!" Priscilla cried. "I'm hurt."

Anna turned away from the blood. "I'll get your sled."

Priscilla was able to stand there on her own, next to Leo. Anna pushed her way through the crowd and got the sled.

"I'll take it," Leo offered.

Priscilla started rubbing her behind. "I did get hurt!" she insisted.

"Priscilla, let's go," Anna said. It sounded loud.

In a line of three, they started down Clark Hill. Anna and her sled were leading. In the middle, Priscilla was shuffling and whimpering. Leo was last, pulling two sleds—his and Priscilla's.

Nobody laughed at them. Anna supposed that meant that Priscilla wasn't still rubbing. But she didn't turn around to see. When they got to the cleared sidewalk, Leo broke the silence. "We can't pull the sleds on the sidewalk," he said. "It would kill the runners."

Priscilla moaned.

"We have to pull on snow," Leo finished.

Anna and Leo McVene together started out, pulling sleds on the bordering snow.

Priscilla was left alone, to walk on the sidewalk. "What if I fall, all by myself, trying to walk?"

"Do you want a ride?" Leo sounded uncertain.

"It's too bumpy." Priscilla was nearly crying again.

"Priscilla, we've got to get home," Anna said. "My mother has to leave for the wake. You walked down the hill. A sidewalk is better than a hill. At least a sidewalk's flat."

"Don't you dare walk fast!"

The procession stopped at corners while Leo carried sleds across the streets, one sled by one sled, and Anna waited with Priscilla because Priscilla said she was scared.

It wasn't dark yet. There was still some winter sunlight. But there was no winter warmth from the sun.

When they got to Anna's house, Leo asked, "Do I take her sled across the street to her house?"

"No," said Priscilla tearfully. "Nobody's home."

"You could leave it right here in front," Anna said. "I'll come back and get it in a minute."

"No!" insisted Priscilla.

"I'll bring it," said Leo.

"Around to the back door," agreed Anna.

"Where people deliver homework," added Leo.

That surprised Anna, and started to be pleasant. But it didn't get to be very pleasant. Priscilla began rubbing her behind again and asked, as though it made her hurt more to have to say the words, "What does that mean? Anna, what does that mean?"

"It means he brought my homework here, yesterday, after school. When I was at Aunt Maria's with you."

Priscilla had the answer, and she didn't want it.

Her question had been automatic, not a question even Priscilla would listen to.

Instead, she was moaning, "I want to go in. I'm sick!"

Ten

It was Priscilla, leaning sideways against the kitchen counter, who told Anna's mother all about the accident. At the end, she said, "I was so darn scared!"

Anna was holding Michael on her lap. His brown eyes were enormous when he turned to look up into Anna's face. The last of the day's light, coming through the kitchen windows, was gray. It gave everyone in the Halder kitchen an unreal look.

Anna kissed Michael's cheek.

Anna's mother said, "Priscilla, I'd better look at your back. Come up to Anna's room. If there are cuts, they should be cleaned."

"Oh no! I hope that won't hurt a lot!"

Priscilla went first as they left the kitchen. She walked slowly and awkwardly.

After a while, Anna's mother returned, alone.

Anna was helping Michael make a domino parade on the kitchen table.

"There aren't any cuts, Anna. But there is an enormous bruise. She asked if you'd go up. I think I'd better not go to the wake."

While Anna was climbing the stairs, she suddenly wondered if she had said good-bye to Leo.

Maybe I did. I was thinking, "Good-bye, Leo. Thank you very much, Leo." Did I say anything? It would have been nice to say something, there at the back door, where people bring homework.

Priscilla was asleep on her side. Anna could hear her breathing deeply and raspingly. Anna could see the streaks made on Priscilla's face by real tears. She closed the bedroom door with authentic care.

It hurts a lot to be that scared. I feel sorry for her. She can't even be in her own bed.

When Anna walked into the kitchen, Michael asked, "Make me some more fall-downs, Anna. Please, in very big lines."

Anna's mother said, "I know she's not seriously hurt, Anna. But I wouldn't feel right going to the wake, leaving you alone. Maybe I'll just call Daddy and tell him not to meet me at the train. I have a right to be tired, I guess." She smiled at Anna.

Is that a lie? Anna wondered. *Not a real one,* she decided. *Not with the way Uncle Charles and Aunt Eleanor would get into a fuss about Priscilla. They'd be fussing, and still at the wake. Fussing about staying there—like they were sure they should.*

Michael and Anna played with the dominoes—and with picture cards of smiling bears—until dinner.

✦   ✦   ✦

Hours later, Uncle Charles heard about the accident. Coming into the house after the wake, with Anna's father, Uncle Charles asked immediately, "Where's Priscilla?"

"Come up, Charles," Anna's mother called softly from the head of the stairs. As he came, she explained about Priscilla's accident, which she called a "fall."

Priscilla was still on Anna's bed. She was lying on her stomach, eating milk toast from a bowl set on a folded bath towel. Priscilla had asked for milk toast. "My mother always gives it to me when I'm sick."

Now Priscilla seemed to be enjoying the milk toast. Anna, who hadn't eaten milk toast since long before Michael was born, was watching and trying to remember if it tasted as slippery as it looked.

Suddenly, even with Uncle Charles' questions coming rapidly, Laurette popped into Anna's head, complete with a Laurette declaration that Anna remembered. "Oatmeal is for babies, Anna. When you have all your teeth, you're supposed to *chew* things."

"My God!" exclaimed Uncle Charles, entering Anna's room. "There might be broken bones! I wish we'd known sooner." He patted Priscilla's head. "I've got to call your mother."

Anna saw her mother shrug.

Aunt Eleanor had gone directly home. She had already undressed for bed. In the time it took her to dress again and pick her way across Hunt Street, Uncle Charles—back in the bedroom, staying near Priscilla—talked to Anna's parents.

"Maria made it stick. She wouldn't go with us to the wake tonight. She won't go to the funeral tomorrow. I think she's unhinged. Eleanor thinks she shouldn't be left alone tomorrow morning. If she won't go to the funeral, she shouldn't sit and brood. Or get more unhinged by looking at torn sheets from Mother's bed and all those old dresses."

"It didn't seem like unhinging to me, Charles," said Anna's father. "It seemed like just a good strong different sort of opinion—the kind that Maria always has, in her own interesting way."

Uncle Charles ignored that. "We were going to ask you," he said to Anna's mother, "to go stay with Maria, during the time of the funeral. Take Michael. We would leave you off there, on the way to the funeral parlor."

"Oh?" Anna's mother made that little sound.

"We'd bring you back. Long before school is over."

The doorbell rang. "Eleanor," said Uncle Charles.

Aunt Eleanor decided instantly that Priscilla had to go to the emergency room at the hospital.

"She probably should have gone right away," she said. "But Rita, I know what you were thinking. About us. Charles and me. Saving us. I might have made the same decision."

She's sounding smarter than my mother.

Anna's mother said calmly, "You'll all feel better, Eleanor, being sure, at the hospital."

Some of the milk spilled onto the towel as Priscilla slid off the bed. Uncle Charles and Aunt Eleanor both helped her stand up.

She groaned. "It hurts."

Anna's mother said, "I don't think anything's broken. You move too well."

"It's her *spine*," countered Aunt Eleanor.

Anna saw a familiar, frightening look cross her mother's face. It was a Johnny look. Anna knew it, and knew what had summoned it. *Little little Johnny had needles in his spine, part of the hospital hurt.*

Uncle Charles asked tensely, "Can she get into her coat?"

The Johnny look vanished. Anna's mother answered, "I should think so. It wouldn't bear heavily on the bruise. And her arms aren't sore."

Uncle Charles hurried ahead to turn on the heater in The Schwannmobile.

Priscilla was bent as she walked out of Anna's room. She seemed to have some real problems stepping down stairs. She held on to the banister and on to her mother, and proceeded the way Michael used to: two feet brought together on one step before there was confidence and courage enough to step with one foot again.

"Ow-w-w!" said Priscilla.

Anna's mother opened the front door for them. She gently kissed Priscilla's cheek.

Aunt Eleanor said, "I can't help thinking about Maria. Nothing happens to Maria. Nothing like this, Rita. You know she's asleep right now. Not a doubt in her mind about the funeral."

They left, Priscilla holding on to her mother and inching along.

Anna immediately went to get undressed. The chapping on her legs was only stiff. Without lotion, by itself, it had stopped stinging. Today's sledding was broken in pieces, and one of the best pieces was lost. Anna felt fleetingly sad and a little bit cheated.

For the second time that day, she wondered if she had said good-bye. She was climbing into her bed, over which a touch of cinnamon smell from Priscilla's milk toast still drifted, thinking, *Did I say, "Good-bye, Priscilla, I hope you feel better"?*

Staring into the darkness for a minute, Anna wondered some more. *Would it do any good if I could just say to them someday, "All you*

Schwanns, don't carry on so much. Please just don't carry on."

She wondered. She wondered hazily.

All of a sudden, she was boneless, being drifted out to sleep.

The next thing she knew, there was a feeling of very early morning, and a peculiar knowledge that, in the funny earliness, it was her mother who was gently shaking her.

"Honey, I need you to wake up. I have to talk to you right away. Charles was just over here."

"In your bathrobe?" Anna asked in her sleep.

"It's me in the bathrobe, Sleepyhead. I hope Charles liked it. I wear it every morning about six o'clock."

"Six o'clock?"

"Really twenty past. Anna, would you go stay with Aunt Maria this morning?"

"Again?" Anna asked, half awake now.

"Different this time. The most important thing—today's your Christmas party at school. You'd be missing that."

Anna's mother waited.

"You don't have to, Anna."

"Stay with Aunt Maria? I don't understand."

"You did hear Uncle Charles talking about it last night? Maria has absolutely decided not to go to the funeral. Charles and Eleanor are worried that she shouldn't be alone today, maybe grieving, all by herself."

"They think she's crazy," Anna said in a flat voice. She was awake now. "That's mean."

Her mother let that comment pass. "You know that I was supposed to take Michael, and go stay with Aunt Maria," she continued. "But then Priscilla got hurt. So Mikey and I are going over there to stay with her. Uncle Charles says she has a hard time moving. Whatever happens, she can't go to the funeral. And I will stay with her. That could leave no one for Maria."

"Me," said Anna.

"You would drive down with the Schwanns. What do you think, Anna?"

Anna said, "I'll go, Mother. I like Aunt Maria. And I don't care a lot about the Christmas party. I know all the answers to the word games anyhow. I'm really too old for parties like that."

"You're just old enough to be exactly right," her mother said.

Anna was standing now.

Her mother went on, "Daddy's leaving about ten to, Anna. Be sure you say good-bye. He has to get his desk cleared—it's such a mixed-up week. I guess I'm glad he'll have a good hour to himself before the funeral."

◆　　　◆　　　◆

Uncle Charles wanted to leave at seven thirty, to be at Aunt Maria's by eight.

Anna was ready early. She had an honorable

couple of minutes to find her father in the kitchen and say good-bye.

"Come see me off, Anna," he said then.

They went to the front door together. When he was ready to leave, he put an arm around Anna's shoulder. "Do you know, Honey? You're making everything possible today. Mother can be with poor old Priscilla. And Charles and Eleanor and I can go to the funeral. Without anybody's worrying too much, in the matter of hinging and unhinging."

Going back to the kitchen, Anna thought, *That's lawyer talk. In-the-matter-of. Someday I could tell him what Laurette thinks about lawyer talk.*

On this funeral morning, that seemed like something honestly bouncy—and something possible. *Maybe I could . . . if ever . . .*

It was a very short breakfast for Anna and her mother. It was a half-asleep one for Michael.

"He looks so funny," Anna whispered. "He's dressed in his clothes. But he's got his pajama face on."

"Take him back to bed." Her mother was whispering, too. "Let him have the last good sleepy minutes before Charles comes."

Back in his bed, Michael turned on his side and began rubbing a circle around the tip of his nose with a forefinger.

"Be happy, Mikey," Anna whispered. "Today's going to be a good day for you. You're going to help Mother take care of Priscilla today, like a big boy. Mother and Priscilla need you. Priscilla fell down. She has to stay in bed. Then, later, I'll come home. And tonight we'll all . . . "

Michael shook his head. His finger moved in a faster circle. Michael didn't want to listen. Not yet, in the morning.

In a second, Anna realized that that was good. It was very good. She rubbed Michael's blond head.

What's the matter with me? Why did I forget? I almost told Michael that we would go to the kids' Christmas party at Priscilla's tonight. I almost told him that he'd remember from last year, about the world's biggest Christmas tree and Michael helping to light it, and all those Christmas cookies. But none of it's true. I'd have to take it all back. He'd cry. Michael would cry, and I could never make him understand. . . . Not this Christmas Eve, Michael. This is Grandmother's funeral day.

Eleven

Uncle Charles rang the bell at seven twenty-five. Anna was pulling Michael's cap down over his ears.

"I'll help with the boy," said Uncle Charles.

Michael offered his mittened hand to Uncle Charles. The four of them crossed Hunt Street, Michael a step ahead of Uncle Charles, but still holding hands.

Michael climbed the Schwann front steps on his own, slowly. Uncle Charles climbed behind Michael, patiently. Aunt Eleanor opened the front door. She started talking at once.

"No broken bones, thank God. You're both real treasures to help today. Poor Priscilla. I don't think she slept much. And—Anna again. I can't believe we're imposing on a child for this. But Maria likes you."

They left almost right away—Uncle Charles,

Aunt Eleanor, Anna, and The Schwannmobile. On the ride, Aunt Eleanor talked a lot. She told about the hospital. She told, on and on, about Priscilla's bruise and Priscilla's pain. Then she was shivering and saying how cold it would be at the cemetery, after the depressing Funeral Mass.

"It's such a mystery to me, that Mass."

Aunt Eleanor fretted about Aunt Maria. "This whole thing may be totally unnecessary, Anna. Taking you out of school again. But you saw Maria the other day. We wonder if she really knows that Grandmother is dead. I just feel that *someone* should be there today. An ear to listen, while the funeral is going on. Maria will talk. She always talks. It couldn't be good if she was just talking to herself."

Uncle Charles spoke. "What if she does decide to go? What do we do with Anna then?"

"She won't go, Charles. I know Maria."

"Well, I'm going to be at her place a half hour early now. I'll try to get her to go. It's her mother as well as mine. She ought to go."

✦   ✦   ✦

They found out that Aunt Maria wouldn't change her mind. Then the three of them sat with Aunt Maria in the apartment living room for a meeting that couldn't end until thirty minutes passed.

Anna kept listening for the striking of a chime

clock, to mark away the fifteen-minute segment.
But Aunt Maria did not have a chime clock—for a
father to forget to wind. Without it, Anna had no
way of knowing how much meeting was left before
Uncle Charles and Aunt Eleanor would finally
leave.

At the end, Aunt Maria was still talking slowly
and glidingly. "I know, Charles dear. But I am not
going. I worked it out years ago. I am not a person
who goes to wakes and funerals."

"How can you say that!" exclaimed Aunt
Eleanor.

"She can say it," said Uncle Charles. "She keeps
saying it. We have to go."

Aunt Maria walked with Uncle Charles and
Aunt Eleanor, down the hall, past the hall tree, to
the door of the apartment. Anna knew every step.

When Aunt Maria came back into the living
room, she smiled. "It's only eight thirty in the
morning," she said. She looked at Anna happily.
Then she looked out the big front windows.
"We're going to have snow!"

The first thing for them to do, Aunt Maria continued, was to frost the Christmas honey cakes.

"I made them early. But a person can't frost
honey cakes until they cool," she explained. She
looked out again. "Isn't it lovely, Anna? Winter,
and Christmas, and honey cakes, and snow."

The smell of the honey cakes was still warm in
the kitchen when they got there. Aunt Maria had

cut the sheets of cake into small, equal brown ob-longs. The big baking pans were soaking in the sink.

The frosting was cream colored, not as white as snow.

"I know why people make honey cakes only at Christmas," Aunt Maria said, frosting delicately. "To keep honey cakes special. They do mean *Christmas*, don't they, Anna?"

"I think it's the smell," Anna answered. "I don't notice spice smells much, except with Christmas baking."

"Windows are open," Aunt Maria remarked, sounding sensible.

Anna smiled, and perked some frosting into a series of small, friendly question marks. She could understand "windows are open."

In the summer, when windows are open, spice smells drift away. All the possible Christmasness goes out the windows, where it belongs. But in winter, windows are closed, and that keeps every-thing inside—which is wonderful when there are good spice smells to trap. They stay inside. They're the Christmas air.

For the next space of time, Anna and Aunt Maria concentrated on frosting. Once in a while, Aunt Maria hummed. Finally, all the honey cakes were ready, capped with frosting.

"When you eat honey cakes, you should always have a party," Aunt Maria said. "We could have a tea party in the living room."

"A tea party? Aunt Maria, I've never been to a tea party."

"Anna! You remember the dresses. It's silly of me to think of this. But they are worthy dresses. And they're so beautiful. And decorative." Aunt Maria's eyebrows went up. "We could," she said, "invite the beautiful dresses to a beautiful party."

They left the frosting alone now, to harden on the honey cakes all by itself. Aunt Maria led the way to the spare bedroom. "Perfect, isn't it, Anna?" she said, over her shoulder. "The dresses will be living Christmas decorations at our party."

"Living" was a shaky word. It kept fluttering in Anna's head while she and Aunt Maria walked down the hall. But it slipped away the minute she saw the dresses again.

Aunt Maria and Anna brought the dresses and the slippers to the living room. Anna carried each dress. Aunt Maria carried each pair of slippers.

The black dress came first. "Black on the sofa nearest the windows," Aunt Maria said. "That will make the buttons sparkle, like Christmas tree ornaments. You'll see. They'll look silver."

The green dress was spread out in the big chair, with its slippers ready. Aunt Maria considered the dress. "Airy," she decided. "That's how the green dress looks."

For the party, Anna was to sit in the center of the sofa, across the room from the yellow dress and its slippers. The yellow dress sat on the little chair beside the painted end table.

Trying out her party place, and looking over to the yellow dress and the yellow slippers, Anna understood something. *Michael would like this party.*

She and Aunt Maria had had a world of make-believe to themselves while they were placing the dresses and the slippers.

It's just like Michael, when he plays with the village. He arranges everything, and he's sure that all of it is real.

Anna expected Aunt Maria to say that it was time to make the tea. But Aunt Maria said, "Wait. I can't help myself. There's something else I want to do."

Aunt Maria wanted to wear her diamond rings to the party. The diamond rings were hidden in the basement, in a drawer of the old dressing table in the storage locker.

"I thought of it when Charles gave me the new keys. I hadn't had anything to do with the old keys for a long time. We hadn't used them in years. We had everything we needed up here already."

"Aunt Maria . . . " Anna edged around her own words so awkwardly that she actually turned her head away from Aunt Maria. "There was probably a robber."

"That's just what I thought, Anna. He tried the locker, and he didn't find anything he wanted. So he wouldn't come back. Also, we had the wonderful new locks, in case he did. I had the fine-looking new keys in my hand. They're so clean, Anna. I looked at the keys, and I could just see the locker door. And the superior places for hiding rings in there."

Now the rings were to come up from the basement, out of hiding, for the honey-cake tea party.

"I don't go down the way Eleanor does," said Aunt Maria. "That just makes it look harder."

They were in the front hall, putting on their coats. Anna looked at herself in the mirror of the hall tree. She saw a person who almost said, *Hide them here again. Aunt Eleanor wouldn't come back here. You figured that out, about the robber. Aunt Eleanor would expect you to change the hiding place.*

Aunt Maria chose to go down the basement by way of the inside front stairs and the building lobby. She pulled open the heavy outside door.

"Anna, look! We're going to have a walk in the first Christmas snow."

The day was gray and frozen. Snow was only half trying to fall. It was a cold walk, around two far-apart corners of the apartment building, all the way to the basement door.

"I hope it's not too cold for a Christmas blizzard," said Aunt Maria.

She pulled the clean keys out of her coat pocket and dangled them for Anna. "You see how different from any old keys they are," she said.

Anna sneezed.

"Poor Anna! The best idea is to get inside quickly."

With the new key in the new lock, opening was very smooth. Aunt Maria and Anna did get inside quickly.

"There!" said Aunt Maria triumphantly. "My rings are right there."

She pointed—full arm extended—at the little dressing table way up, on top of the chest of drawers that was set on the canvas-covered table inside the locker.

"Such really nice keys," Aunt Maria said to herself, opening the locker door now.

She pulled out one of the chairs that were stored under the banquet table. She backed the chair against the table and climbed onto it. Standing there, Aunt Maria could reach directly up—over her head—to the center drawer of the dressing table, and open it. She couldn't see into it.

Anna watched as Aunt Maria's hand moved back and forth inside the drawer.

"That's funny," she said. "I don't feel my rings."

The furnace wasn't safely far away, in some remote room of the basement. It shot out a gulp of noise now, close to the locker. There were rumblings and loud rattlings, some in the wall behind the dressing table.

"Did you find your rings?" Anna's voice was shaky.

Over her shoulder, Aunt Maria looked down. "Did that furnace scare you, Anna? It is a startle, I'll admit. But it's a very fine furnace. Although

Charles thinks it costs too much."

What would Charles think about a robber stealing Grandmother's rings?

Turning back to the drawer, Aunt Maria was definitely calm. "The thing to do," she said, "is to tip the drawer a little forward. When I pushed it closed, the rings must have shot backward. That's reasonable."

It wasn't possible to tip the drawer. Aunt Maria decided to take a sidewise step. "I'll paw around from the side. I'll be able to reach better, I think."

Anna heard Aunt Maria's hand pawing in the drawer.

"Ah! One ring. I'll just put it on for safe keeping."

She found the second ring right after that, and put it on, too.

Now the furnace sighed inward. Aunt Maria could not find the third ring.

She brought her arm down. She sighed. "Of course it's in here. But it's stubborn."

Renewed, she asked Anna to climb up to the canvas surface, too, on the other side of the opened drawer.

"The two of us. We'll just tip the whole dressing table forward. And the ring will slide right down here to the front of the drawer."

Anna climbed to the canvas surface. They agreed on the way they would tip the dressing table. They agreed that they were ready to tip.

They tipped.

There was a loud splintering sound.

Anna's side of the dressing table tilted, down toward its broken front leg. Anna held on. She stopped the whole dressing table from collapsing to the concrete floor of the storage locker.

"Don't fall, Anna! Let it slide. I'll never miss it. Not if it breaks into a hundred pieces. Oh my!"

"Aunt Maria, it's important. Get the ring. I'm all right."

The little dressing table wasn't heavy, even forcing most of its weight into Anna's hands. But why was it taking so long, over there, on Aunt Maria's side? The drawer was certainly tipped now. Anna thought that she could hear a ring on Aunt Maria's hand hitting on the wooden drawer bottom as Aunt Maria tried to paw over the whole area.

"It is not here. It is simply not here."

"Aunt Maria, I'll put my side all the way down to the chest of drawers. It should prop up the whole dressing table."

Anna was right. In its curious position, the little table seemed solid.

"I'll get down first, Aunt Maria."

"Where could my ring be?"

Anna helped Aunt Maria climb down.

They stood and looked up helplessly at the entire drawer, now hanging out of the table.

It's only one thing lost. But it's a DIAMOND RING lost.

The big heavy words "diamond ring" pressed on Anna. She lowered her head.

She saw the third ring. It was near a front leg of the climbing chair. A round cluster of diamond circles, it didn't look valuable. It just looked heavy.

"Oh I am so glad!" said Aunt Maria. "Of course! It fell out during the splintering, and we didn't hear it hit. Anna, Anna! That silly ring! I am so done in, chasing rings!"

She said that they had to sit and rest, right there in the storage locker, on the stored chairs, with the furnace declaring like a trusted old guardian in the background.

Anna brought out another chair. She slumped, but Aunt Maria didn't. Sitting up straight, Aunt Maria looked at her hands. Ready-to-play-the-piano hands, with three rings to shine in the stage lights.

"It's too dim here. They don't show up properly," she said dreamily. "They have the liveliest sparkle. Particularly when Mother's hands moved. Even eating soup. Sparkling. Anna, try on one of my rings."

Anna sat up. Aunt Maria offered her the third ring.

The ring was big on Anna's finger—the size surprisingly too large. The stones together crowded like a walnut under her knuckle. She and Aunt Maria each silently considered sparkle for a little while.

"You have to be sensible about diamonds," said Aunt Maria. "I should think that, if you have too many, you would get impatient with them. Tired of them. All of them essentially the same. Like stones in a bucket."

A bucket of diamonds. Anna grinned.

Aunt Maria was still posing her hands. "Anna, what do you think about that King of England?" she asked.

She had to mean Edward, last month's King of England. Sister Elizabeth had fit Edward into seventh-grade lessons one morning, a little while ago, after the excitement of the King's abdication. Sister had talked about the long line of British monarchs, each following the last, in something like a parade of noble burden bearers. Their line stretched richly and movingly into infinity, where it dissolved on the leading end.

King Edward had faltered and dropped out of the solemn line. He walked away, to marry Mrs. Simpson, the woman he loved. She was not an acceptable woman to be queen, to walk next to her husband, with full dignity, in the line. Mrs. Simpson had been—as a queen must never be—divorced.

What did Anna think about that King of England? Anna thought that the news about him was chillingly romantic. But she wished that Mrs. Simpson were prettier, more like a princess.

Anna didn't have time to say any of this. Aunt

Maria was continuing. "He should have thought. You cannot make a Mrs. into a queen of England. It would have been so unwholesome. What if one of her husbands came to a party?" Aunt Maria pondered that. She added, "By mistake."

They're bumping into each other—everybody at the party. They're trying to get the extra husband out of the palace. Aunt Maria, Aunt Maria. You do mean it! And I am not going to laugh!

"He's gone now, Anna," said Aunt Maria. "He crept away. That's not kingly. I wish my mother knew about it. She would have had something to say."

Aunt Maria was finished with Edward. Returned to rings, she said, "These are very new to me personally, Anna. Although I did know they'd sometime be mine. Mother always told me. Right now, I think I want to wear them all the time. Even when I'm knitting rags. Anna, I do want to try knitting rags with my diamonds."

Now it was Aunt Maria who leaned back. She didn't look slumpy, just relaxed.

"As I remember, when I was learning to knit, everything seemed yellow. Not as bright as diamonds. Not nearly as bright. But beautiful."

Aunt Maria held up her hands to look at the first ring and the second ring. They were still not sparkling properly. The basement simply didn't have any kind of light strong enough to tease the best sparkle out of diamonds. Aunt Maria shook her head lovingly at the rings, and resumed talking.

"We were in Michigan." Aunt Maria folded her hands in her lap. "In the dunes. We went there most summers when we were little. You stayed in a boarding house. Everyone did. There were no hotels. The dunes were wild. Your footprints didn't stay in them for a minute. I used to think that maybe the dunes didn't want you to climb them. Sometimes the sand grabbed your feet and held on. It was work to get free. Don't you think that meant, Anna, that the dunes didn't want anybody to get to the top? And see the private other side that they had hidden, maybe since the dinosaurs, and how it eased down and turned into the sand of the beach? And there was the lake, far ahead, beyond the beach. Such a blue lake. With yellow sunlight over it that was so clear. It looked . . . " Aunt Maria smiled—at herself, Anna could tell—and said, "It looked *original*."

Original. Aunt Maria kept smiling about the impossible sunlight of that funny word.

"You have been to the dunes, Anna?"

"Two times. I went with Priscilla." Same Priscilla. Same Uncle Charles and Aunt Eleanor. Not The Schwannmobile, yet. "There was a staircase up the front of one dune. At first, I thought it was a scaffold—that they were making a dune. But it was only a staircase. To help people climb."

"A silly staircase," said Aunt Maria. "Mrs. Parrot would have laughed at it. Mrs. Parrot was our

boardinghouse lady, Anna. For summers after
summers. She is the one who taught me to knit
rags. On the porch. In the yellow sunshine there. I
have never remembered to ask if that was her
proper name. Was she really Mrs. Parrot? Or was
that only what I heard when the grown-ups were
talking?"

Now Aunt Maria was quiet, wondering about
that. Now Anna was quiet, trying to form a picture
of Mrs. Parrot in the sunshine.

Aunt Maria said clearly, "I'd like to ask my
mother."

I'd like to ask my mother. Anna was startled.
She clutched at the big third ring. While it was biting the back of her finger, she heard Uncle
Charles' distinct complaint about Aunt Maria, "I
think she's unhinged."

*Would a hinged Aunt Maria say a thing like that
right now? I'd like to ask my mother? On her
mother's funeral day, exactly while her mother is
being buried in the ground?*

"Oh Aunt Maria!" The sounds spilled out. Anna
wasn't sure that they were even words.

"Are you sick, Anna?" Aunt Maria sat up. "Are
you suddenly sick?" She reached toward Anna.
She tried to look into her face.

With ridiculous downward care, staring at her
diamond cluster, Anna said, "I was thinking about
Grandmother."

Aunt Maria took Anna's hand, the plain one,

without the diamond ring. "Anna dear," she said gently, "I've been talking about the good times in Michigan. Of course that would remind you that my mother had been there. And now she's dead. Just a few days ago." Aunt Maria waited for a little while. "I'm sorry to have done this, Anna. What I forgot was that very young people like you—the best of young people, like you, the most kindly, like you—think that death is just hurtful, and that dead bodies are sad." She squeezed Anna's hand. "You were thinking of how my mother would have been, at the wake. Pasty faced. It's no wonder you felt bad, nearly sick. Flowers smell so awful at wakes. A person wouldn't recognize them."

It was steadying, in the warm basement—with the winter held outside and the furnace massively at work inside—to have a hand held by Aunt Maria. It didn't feel unhinged when Aunt Maria patted that hand, then started playing uncertain piano notes on the back of it.

"I don't know everything in the world about death, Anna. A person can't know. Sometimes it does seem all hurtful. But the dead person isn't totally gone. Because you can concentrate. And there are lovely living things to remember." Aunt Maria hesitated, pausing also in the piano notes on Anna's hand. The notes quickly picked up, like a march.

When they died away, the march feeling was left behind. "About dead bodies. . . . Charles would say I'm stubborn, and he has a right to say that. I don't go to wakes. They are parties for bodies."

Anna saw a smooth flush on Aunt Maria's cheeks. "As for my mother," Aunt Maria was finishing, "she is no different than other dead people. My mother is important without her body. My mother doesn't need her body anymore."

That body, incredibly light, wafted away from anything Anna had to think about. There was nothing here connected to craziness, to anyone's being unhinged. But there was a connection to Johnny. Anna knew that right away. It was a connection that felt light immediately—and yellow, like dunes in sunlight.

Johnny doesn't need his body anymore. It doesn't matter—all the hospital hurt. Johnny is important, for me and my mother, without remembering the hurt. . . . There are so many lovely Johnny things to remember.

We can tell Daddy.

Anna couldn't thank Aunt Maria because Anna couldn't be sensible and clear and calm yet, in explaining this to anyone. She was quiet, but she felt as though she were laughing—an inside laughing, about something like the yellow sun coming out in April.

"My goodness my gracious!" exclaimed Aunt Maria. "We'd better be rested by now, Anna. We don't have much more time. And we have our whole tea party to celebrate."

They put the chairs back under the table. Aunt Maria gave the dressing table some thought, looking up at it from two different spots in the storage locker.

"We can't repair it," she said. "It might have fallen like that, by itself. Who would ask? They know that old wood dries out."

She shrugged her shoulders.

Michael does that when he doesn't want to tell the truth about something naughty that has been traced to him.

"Button all the way up, Anna. We'll be especially cold, coming up out of the basement."

Twelve

It was comfortingly warm in the apartment. They hung their coats on the fingers of the hall tree. Anna was still wearing the third ring. She stood in front of the hall tree and watched the diamonds' mirrored sparkle as she moved her hand. It was another way to see the rapid changing movements of light around the ring.

"I told you about the sparkle, Anna," Aunt Maria said. "Now that we're in the middle of the hall lights, you see the sparkle."

They both looked at sparkle another minute, then went to set the party on the long coffee table in the living room. The setting included a dinner plate with honey cakes, the Irish teapot with sugar bowl and creamer, china cups and saucers, small dessert plates, and silverware.

Anna took her party seat in the center of the velvet sofa. Aunt Maria sat—facing the big windows—on the loveseat that was precisely set across the end of the coffee table.

"It all has to wait a minute," Aunt Maria said, jumping up. "I forgot the napkins."

Coming back into the living room, she said, "There! We're elegant now. The lace around these napkins is tatting. You can't do that by machine. Anna, I'm nearly sure that Mrs. Parrot did this tatting for us."

The party began. The dresses were ornaments if a person shut her eyes and saw that the whole living room was a supreme Christmas tree. Or— the dresses were Christmas trees themselves, made of colored cellophane wound into tubes and then fluffed out. The slippers were the most interesting ornaments. Or—they were simply fairy-tale twelve-o'clock-midnight slippers, made of glass.

Anna put her cup down slowly. She looked at the third diamond ring. *I have diamonds, at a tea party.*

"I hope you like this party," Aunt Maria said softly. "I know you missed your party at school. Eleanor told me you would. She told me many times, this morning, on the phone, when your mother couldn't come. And they didn't want me to be alone. And"—she smiled over her teacup—"I didn't want to be alone." She took a sip of tea. "I do make good tea," she said. "Celebrating makes this tea even better, don't you think, Anna?" Aunt Maria finished with another question. "I hope the illness has moderated. Do you know?"

Anna was puzzled. "I don't know, Aunt Maria. Do bruises do that? Do bruises moderate?"

"Bruises? Did he fall? Poor Michael. I supposed he had a bad winter cold."

Michael was not sick. Some strong pulse from Johnny's July made Anna insist on that. Instantly, without considering anything, she said emphatically, "Not Michael. It's Priscilla."

"Priscilla? Oh, I didn't listen correctly. What's the matter with Priscilla? A cold, too?"

Anna told about Priscilla's lifesaving fall on Clark Hill. She told it seriously enough, and Aunt Maria was seriously interested.

Anna didn't say "behind."

Aunt Maria summed up the story. "Priscilla bumped her butt."

Anna tried not to laugh. Aunt Maria winked, distinctly, mischievously, and without meanness. They both laughed, a little—not the kind of laughing that would hurt Priscilla's feelings.

"The rest of Priscilla's story is elegant enough for our party, Anna. A beautiful snow-covered hill. The old-fashioned sport of sledding. Aristocratic. The gallant young man who helped the injured lady and the young-lady companion on their way home. Yes." She nodded. "Very elegant."

"He didn't really have to help Priscilla." Anna wanted to make that definite.

But Aunt Maria was already thinking of something entirely else. "Anna . . . when we were little, we used to play Change Your Name. It wasn't a real game. No one but a few of us little girls played it. We'd say 'What name would you have now, if you'd picked it out for yourself at the beginning?' My, but I did go through a lot of changes of name. Once, someone told me I should be Wisteria. And I thought about that for a long time. Would you think of Wisteria for yourself, Anna?"

"Wisteria Halder. It sounds funny, Aunt Maria."

"Oh, I agree. I do agree. But Anna, you have to admit, Wisteria is elegant."

"What was your best name, Aunt Maria?"

Aunt Maria put her cup down. She looked out the windows, peacefully, into the air that had been there since she was a little girl, picking out names.

"You'll never believe, Anna. I ran all around, with Wisteria trailing after, looking for my best name. When I found it, I knew I wanted it. I would be Marie. One letter different. But very elegant, and modern. Isn't it elegant, Anna? Just *a* changed to *e*?"

Anna saw right away that there could be that wonderful elegance for her, too. She said, "I could do the same thing, Aunt Maria."

"Anna. Anne. Yes, you could. *A* changed to *e*."

"Aunt Maria, it does make a difference."

Anne. A big difference. Anne, mature and thin. Stylish, even in her uniform, a high-school uniform. Four years of high school. Going to proms at the boys' school. Anne Halder going with Leo McVene.

"Anna is a beautiful name," said Aunt Maria. "I shouldn't make you dissatisfied with it. I'm just so surprised that it is exactly as adaptable as mine. The same way."

Anne left. Anna spoke. "I suppose lots of names are like that."

"One isn't," Aunt Maria said, with unashamed mischievousness. "Priscilla isn't."

"Priscilla . . . Priscille. You're right, Aunt Maria. What does that sound like? Priscille. A country. Priscille-Brazil."

"It sounds to me," said Aunt Maria, "like the old-fashioned material you made your under-clothes with. I think there might have been a material like that. Or Priscille could be an Italian noodle." She thought about that. "Before you cook it," she added.

The doorbell rang. Aunt Maria jumped up. "Is it over already! I'll have to let them in."

Grandmother's funeral was finished. Uncle Charles and Aunt Eleanor were waiting at the door. The dresses were sitting in the living room, pretending to wear their slippers. For half a second, Anna felt like snatching the dresses away and running with them, back to the spare bedroom. But even if she could carry them, all three at once, she would have to come back for the slippers.

Rushing them down the hall, she would meet

Uncle Charles and Aunt Eleanor face to face. Everyone would stop. They would stare at Anna— her arms full of slippers that couldn't be explained.

Anna sat still on the velvet sofa and heard Aunt Eleanor exclaim, "They couldn't put the casket in the ground!"

Uncle Charles stopped in the hall bathroom. Aunt Eleanor strode directly into the living room. Aunt Maria followed—a long way back, it seemed to Anna.

"What is this?" demanded Aunt Eleanor. "What is this absurd thing?"

Anna didn't answer. She felt as though she waited two full hours before Aunt Maria, coming into the living room, did answer.

"The dresses were very wrinkled," said Aunt Maria.

"What do wrinkles matter! Honestly, Maria! This is a funeral day, for all of us, even relatives who chose not to be there." She turned from Aunt Maria. She relaxed her lips. She shook her head. She said to Anna, "I really *can* tell, Anna, that you are not one of Maria's old dresses. I'm sorry she got me so upset that I didn't say hello to you right away. Has it been a very bad morning here, Anna?"

Behind Aunt Eleanor, Aunt Maria shrugged. She was like Michael, again, determined not to be caught being naughty.

"No, Aunt Eleanor, it hasn't been bad."

"Bad what?" asked Uncles Charles, coming into the living room.

Aunt Eleanor turned—not all the way toward Uncle Charles. With no gesturing at all, Aunt Eleanor said, "Charles. Look."

Uncles Charles looked—slowly from the yellow dress to the green dress to the black dress. Anna was aware that his head was turning, but she didn't raise her eyes fully, to see his face.

"Yes." On that unexpected, vague sound, Uncle Charles walked over to the sofa. He sat down next to Anna, making three in a row: the black dress, Anna, himself.

"Yes WHAT?" demanded Aunt Eleanor.

"Yes, I see the dresses. Maria was showing them off, I suppose."

There were a lot of esses in Uncle Charles' reply. Around the esses was an unpleasant odor.

"Well, for heaven's sake, Charles. This kind of sideshow? This is a funeral day, Charles. For all of us!"

"They were mother's dresses," said Aunt Maria.

Anna wanted to say something, to help explain the dresses. But right then, Anna couldn't remember how to swallow and get started talking.

"It wasn't a funeral day, complete," said Uncle Charles, looking down at his hands. "I didn't know," he continued, very slowly, "that they couldn't dig a grave in this weather."

Bitter cold.

"What does that matter here?" asked Aunt Eleanor sharply.

Uncle Charles went on, talking slowly to his hands. "They can't get a shovel into the ground."

He suddenly looked toward Anna. "Did you mind the dresses?" he asked.

With those last few esses, Anna could identify the odor. Uncle Charles had thrown up.

He passed a hand over his mouth, pulling his chin down.

Then he said, "I guess you didn't mind."

"Charles, did you expect her to say so? She and Priscilla—girls this age don't tattle." Then Aunt Eleanor turned to Anna and invited her to tattle. "What else went on here, Anna?"

Anna answered shakily, "We baked honey cakes. I mean—we frosted honey cakes." Aunt Eleanor was staring at her. "For Christmas."

"Honey cakes!" exclaimed Aunt Eleanor. "I dare you to tell that to anyone, Charles. 'My mother was being buried and my sister was home, baking honey cakes.' She didn't have to bake them this year, Charles. It certainly isn't a regular year, for the children's party."

Uncle Charles lowered his head into his hands. It was so surprising a move that no one said a word, although Anna could feel in the air that Aunt Eleanor wanted to go on.

She'll go on and on. She'll find out about how Aunt Maria hid the rings.

Uncle Charles' voice was muffled but under-standable. "Mother wasn't buried. I can still see the casket. On the table there. In the tent. A tent. She'll wait until April, or May. What will happen? What kind of thing is that!"

He sounded as though he were crying. There were probably tears in Uncle Charles' eyes.

He thinks Grandmother is lonesome. He thinks she is left behind, abandoned. He thinks Grand-mother is frightened.

Now Anna looked at Aunt Maria. *Tell him. Tell about dead bodies.*

Aunt Maria did, softly, without advancing a step. "Charles, it doesn't matter. Mother doesn't need her body anymore."

Aunt Eleanor exploded. She made the air shake. "That's ghoulish! Have you been talking like that to ANNA! Her baby brother died, you know!"

Aunt Eleanor screamed louder about this than about the rings hidden in the hall tree.

Uncle Charles raised his head. "They didn't tell us to expect it. It didn't end. I thought it would be all over." Then he looked at Anna, as though he had just awakened, and she was there.

"You're tired, Charles," whispered Aunt Maria. "And Mother died."

Shaken, Anna stared at the yellow dress. She tried desperately to redesign parts of it.

The sash should be wider. More material in the

skirt. More petals for the tulip shape of the skirt.

It didn't work.

Anna wanted to yell, at all of them. She had to press her lips together, so tightly that they felt like lips with bones inside, so that she wouldn't yell.

Don't anybody talk about people dying. Don't talk about Johnny anymore.

Aunt Eleanor said, "Anna. I can't apologize enough. I should have stayed here myself."

She was going to say more. But her eyes suddenly saw the diamond ring, big as coal, on Anna's finger.

"My God in Heaven, Maria!" she exclaimed. "You really are unhinged! You can't give that ring away!"

"She didn't, Aunt Eleanor." It was now hard for Anna not to yell. "Aunt Maria didn't give it to me. She just let me wear it awhile."

Aunt Eleanor didn't want to hear that. "I told you about the rings, Charles. They had to take that ring out of a boot. Out of a galosh. Maria hides all the rings there. IN A GALOSH!"

"I do not." Anna heard again Aunt Maria's special voice for ring fighting. "I do not put my mother's rings in the hall tree anymore."

Uncle Charles looked at the ring on Anna's hand. "She didn't give it to Anna," he said tonelessly. "And Anna's going to give it back." Uncle Charles looked up—at Anna's face, one look. He shook his head. "She's upset enough," he said, far away.

"Anna gives the ring back, of course, Charles."
Aunt Eleanor was scolding. "That doesn't solve
anything. Don't you understand? Somebody has
got to take care of the rings. Do you want them to
be lost?"

"I won't," said Aunt Maria.

"Everyone's screaming," said Uncle Charles.
"How could Maria lose the rings? She's always
here."

He stood. He walked out of the living room,
leaving them. They heard him open the hall bathroom door and shut it behind himself.

Aunt Eleanor turned, full face, to Aunt Maria.
"I'm just as upset as Charles is. By the funeral, and
not being able to carry on with the burial. I wasn't
prepared for this—the dresses and all. Maria, it
looks garish. And completely insensitive. I'll try to
think that that is only the way it looks, that the
whole thing is kind of a silly memorial to Grandmother. You have to see my side of this, Maria."

Anna stood up. She took a few steps and put the
third diamond ring in Aunt Maria's hand. Aunt
Maria closed her fingers over the ring. She hugged
Anna. She patted her back with one flat palm and
one diamond fist. She whispered, "Thank you for
coming. Anne." She repeated the whispered
name. "Anne."

Aunt Eleanor embraced Aunt Maria. They were
two ladies the same size, looking like partners who
didn't know each other.

"It's been a difficult day, Maria," Aunt Eleanor said firmly.

From the vicinity of the hall tree, Uncle Charles called back to the living room, "Let's get going."

Thirteen

During this Schwannmobile ride home, a full blizzard threatened in the gray sky. The lake was only sullen. The Pier had given up. It didn't try to look even faintly beautiful. It merely endured, slapped by waves and dirtied.

In the backseat, Anna sat near the window, with the plaid blanket folded over her knees. She put her elbow on the armrest and held up her chin. She couldn't see anything as warm as Christmas in the world outside the window.

I'd like to be little as Michael. No one paying any attention to me. Just Daddy reading to me A Child's Garden of Verses at night. Little as that.

Finally, the ride was over.

While Aunt Eleanor was hurrying to the Schwann front door, Uncle Charles waited. He waited, and watched, while Anna climbed out of the backseat. He nodded. Anna followed him up the steps to his front door.

As soon as Michael saw Anna, he ran to her and hugged her leg as tightly as he could. She tried to pick him up, wanting to hold him. He resisted, clinging strongly. In one minute, he yielded.

Anna held him tightly. "You're a nice sack of Michael," she whispered.

Aunt Eleanor was talking. "I have never understood how we non-Catholics should take that Funeral Mass. It's drear. As often as I've seen it. Incense is such an awful smell. Is it supposed to frighten you? They couldn't bury the body. We're so upset about that."

Anna's mother said, "I'm so sorry, Eleanor."

Aunt Eleanor explained the frozen cemetery ground.

Anna's mother shook her head in sympathy.

"A dreadful thing," said Aunt Eleanor.

Then Anna's mother was able to say, "Hello, Anna."

Priscilla called from upstairs, "Mother! How was the funeral?"

"Poor thing!" exclaimed Aunt Eleanor.

"She's been fine, Eleanor. She's been playing with Michael."

Priscilla couldn't. She doesn't know how.

"Mother!" called Priscilla.

"Go on up, Eleanor. Say good-bye for me. We really did have a good morning."

This time, it was three Halders who were

escorted across Hunt Street by Uncle Charles.

He carried Michael. Michael burrowed, because it was cold. Michael stayed burrowed, because he was sleepy and—Anna knew—feeling safe, on Uncle Charles' shoulder.

Inside the front door, Uncle Charles stood, holding his hat. He seemed to be studying the way a person, such as Anna's mother, gets a limp three-year-old, such as Michael, out of winter wraps when he is swaying on his feet.

Why does he care? Why does he stay? And not go?

Uncle Charles didn't move.

"Excuse me, Charles. He has to go to nap now," said Anna's mother. Michael's head was already asleep on her shoulder. "I'll be down soon. If you want to stay."

He wants to talk to me. That felt final, and alarming. *Uncle Charles is waiting to talk to me.*

Anna's mother carried Michael up the stairs. Anna and Uncle Charles heard Michael's door close.

"Now. Anna. Maria is fine. There, in the apartment. There's nothing the matter with her. She has too much imagination."

Now Uncle Charles was studying his hat. "And people say the wrong things. When they're out of kilter. When there's something like a funeral."

Is my mother singing to Michael?

"It will straighten out," Uncle Charles continued.

"It will calm down. When we get used to every-thing." Uncle Charles put his hat on his head and his hand on the doorknob. "Thank you, in any case, Anna. Although I wasn't sure you should go. Let Maria be alone, I said. Stubborn enough." Uncle Charles paused. "That part about dead bod-ies. I told Eleanor there would be something like that. Not for children."

This was a lesson that Uncle Charles was study-ing out loud, with his hat on his head. He finished, "Especially not—Eleanor is right—because The Baby Here died."

The stiff and serious hat was black. Under the depth of it, Uncle Charles' eyes disappeared, and his face got darker. He opened the door and stepped out into the cold.

"Uncle Charles, he is not The Baby Here," Anna declared, very loudly, after him. "Don't call Johnny The Baby Here. He still has his name. He is Johnny, Uncle Charles."

The declaration declared itself. Anna was shaken to hear it. It ended in a quaver.

Uncle Charles turned around. He said, slowly and sadly, "Yes, Anna."

Uncle Charles pulled the door closed. The noise was loud in the cold hall.

Michael's door opened and closed with very small sounds. Anna's mother came down the stairs. *Past Johnny's picture.* She stopped near Anna.

"Were you calling Uncle Charles back, Anna?

From across the street?" she asked.

"He forgot his hat," Anna lied quickly.

"Charles?" her mother questioned. "In this weather?"

"It isn't snowing yet."

"It will," said her mother. "Have some lunch with me?"

"I had some. With Aunt Maria."

"It was a pretty calm morning?"

"Probably like yours." This felt like another lie, because it was such a slight account of the morning. "We had honey cakes."

Her mother said, "I always think of Maria's honey cakes in advance. When it's coming to be Christmas Eve and time for your Christmas party, I always get hungry for them, even if I am a grown-up. Yes, right now. I'm hungry for honey cakes."

"But there won't be a party tonight, Mother," Anna said. "Grandmother just . . . "

Her mother kissed Anna's cheek, interrupting. "Priscilla assured me that there will be a party. Her mother promised her—in the emergency room. Because Priscilla was still hurting so much. And because Anna missed her school party. Priscilla said all of that." She added, "You know, Daddy will be home early—this day without fail, Anna. It is a Christmas party day after all. The party is tonight, wonderfully as usual, Anna."

✦   ✦   ✦

Wonderfully as usual. Anna walked into her room, wishing everything wasn't as usual, wishing for no party at all.

She looked at her bedroom clock. A little more than four hours to pass—then, the party as usual.

Maybe I could get really sick and not have to go.

She stepped onto her rag rug and said out loud, "Grow up, Anna Halder."

Anna sat down at her desk. NO, she wrote on a piece of new notebook paper. *Grow down. Get so little that Uncle Charles won't be able to see you.*

She doodled a little bug-sized Anna near a big shoe, which belonged to Uncle Charles.

Right away, she wrote—next to the dumb little bug—NOT FUNNY.

Not funny at all. I have to go to the party. Uncle Charles will complain, "That girl yelled at me."

Anna put her head down on her crossed arms. She almost napped, but the weight of her head made her arms numb. Anna stirred and plodded over to her bed.

She fell asleep. And stayed asleep until Michael came. Michael was shaking Anna's shoulder. Saying, "Wake up, Anna. Comb your hair. I'm waking you up."

Anna sleepily reached over to hug Michael. He dodged away. Anna sat up.

Michael was standing out of her reach, hands on his hips. He looked like a well-dressed big doll. The well-dressed doll reminded Anna right away. The last of her sleepiness vanished.

The party as usual. At Uncle Charles' house. I yelled at Uncle Charles.

"Comb your hair," Michael repeated, and ran from Anna's room.

✦   ✦   ✦

The serious snowstorm had started while Anna slept. As the Halders crossed Hunt Street, it was still only a snowstorm—not as big as a blizzard.

"This is going to be a blizzard," said Anna's father.

Carried in his father's arms, Michael declared, "I can shovel lots of snow!"

I wish someone would carry me, in his pocket, and forget that I was there.

Aunt Eleanor opened the front door before Anna's mother could ring the bell.

"I've been watching for you," she announced. "This is such a special party tonight."

Priscilla was lying on the couch, on her side. She was facing the real fireplace with the real fire burning in it.

Uncle Charles was sitting in the Uncle Charles chair, near the front window that looked past the Schwann porch straight over Hunt Street to the Halder house. Uncle Charles, in that rocking chair, was always ready to look over, to the house . . .

. . . *where she yelled. That is where Anna yelled at me.*

In the blue armless chair near the fireplace, looking directly at the front door, sat Aunt Maria.

Her hands were fingertip-folded on her lap. Anna saw firelight burnishing the diamond rings. She saw little firelight jumps around the big diamonds.

"Maria. How great you look!" said Anna's father. "You're sparkling like Christmas."

"She had to come," Priscilla said. "She always comes. Even if it's snowing."

"Priscilla sobbed," said Aunt Eleanor. "When I told her that Maria wouldn't be here because of the blizzard. Maria is just part of the Christmas party. Charles had to make the trip back in the snow, to get Maria. We should have thought about the blizzard. When we were there, at Maria's. She'll stay tonight."

"That's a powerful car," Uncle Charles said. "Even in snow."

Aunt Maria, being Schwannmobiled to the party. With the honey cakes. Not mad at anybody. Really happy to be riding through the snow. Probably wishing it was a blizzard already.

"Here I am," said Aunt Maria.

"Merry Christmas," said Michael surprisingly.

"What a good boy," exclaimed Aunt Eleanor. "I think he wants to sing 'Jingle Bells.'"

"Get the lights ready first," said Aunt Maria.

Uncle Charles said, "The lights are ready. They always are ready."

If there was a complaint in that, Anna didn't hear it.

I hope Uncle Charles really likes this party, and the carols, and the tree, and the Christmas blizzard coming. And then he will forget about whoever yelled at him.

Aunt Eleanor got ready to play. The printed music was waiting on the upright piano. Branches of the dark Christmas tree nearly touched the piano. Other branches rose to the ceiling, a motiony tent beside the piano.

The first song was "Jingle Bells."

Michael sat on his mother's lap, sidewise. He watched her mouth singing, and sometimes he sang, too.

Aunt Eleanor went on playing, carol after carol. Aunt Maria sang. Priscilla sang. Uncle Charles kept time with his foot. Once in a while, he said some of the words. Anna sang. She heard her father singing, very softly.

It was a slow Ferris wheel ride upward of singing. They got close to the top.

Uncle Charles rose and crossed to Michael. He lifted him carefully from his mother's lap. Hand in hand, Uncle Charles and Michael went to the space between the piano and the Christmas tree. Uncle Charles picked up the end of the tree's electric cord and handed it to Michael. Michael crept into the space. Uncle Charles bent close to Michael. Aunt Eleanor started playing "Silent Night." She played softly, for their very, very soft singing.

On "All is bright," the dark tree disappeared. Its space was filled with BRIGHT—lights and ornament glows and tinsel shine.

They finished singing this last carol. Michael clapped. Everyone clapped.

"Michael did a good job," said Uncle Charles.

"I'm alofted," said Aunt Maria.

"Let's open presents," said Priscilla.

Fourteen

Anna sat on the floor and helped Priscilla with her presents. There were five of them tonight, in party tradition. It was always and unchangingly a children's party. At these Christmas Eve parties now, Anna and Priscilla and Michael received the gifts—from each other, from Aunt Maria, and from the opposite set of parents.

Anna mainly collected torn wrappings from Priscilla's presents. There was a tiny box from Aunt Maria. There was a chess set from Anna's father. Priscilla read out the gift card: "Guess who might be the King Charles of chess players? He'll teach you. And then I'll beat you. Love, from Uncle Justin." Anna's mother gave Priscilla a cream-colored bathrobe. "It's the color of milk toast!" Priscilla exclaimed. Everyone laughed, Michael joining in.

Michael gave Priscilla a bicycle basket.

"Wow, Michael," said Priscilla. "How did you know I needed this?"

"I didn't," said Michael.

Priscilla laughed. "You're a noodle, Michael."

Michael happily hid his face in his mother's lap. He had been opening his presents there, staying as close as possible to his mother, but holding up each present for his father to see.

"Michael Noodle," his father said now. "You get great presents, you dear old Christmas Noodle!"

It crossed Anna's mind to wonder if the high-top boots would be a present—with a knife pocket, and taller than everything else—when Priscilla opened her Christmas-morning packages from her parents. She hoped that the boots wouldn't make Priscilla forget forever how perfect the thin gold cross and chain from Aunt Maria was.

Holding her last present, the one from Anna, Priscilla said, "I can feel what's inside. Books. You pick out such good books, Anna. But don't tell me about them. I want to find out for myself. Now you open your presents."

From Aunt Eleanor to Anna, there was a white sweater set that Anna instantly liked very much. From Priscilla, a school bag with three compartments inside and two snap pockets outside. From Michael, a book Sister Elizabeth had read from in literature class, *Poems for Young People*.

"Michael, did you listen," Anna asked with mock seriousness, "when I was reading the library book out loud?"

"No," answered Michael.

From Aunt Maria to Anna there was the apple-red-and-bright-green rag rug.

"For Christmastimes on your floor," Aunt Maria said happily.

And then, from Uncle Charles, a purse. It was a small leather purse, pleated in front, quietly polished, lilac—one of the greatest colors Anna had ever seen.

She looked at the gift card again. "Merry Christmas" was printed at the top. In the open white space beneath, "Anna. From Uncle Charles" was not in Aunt Eleanor's writing.

"It's a beautiful purse," Aunt Maria said. "I told Charles about the shop. But I didn't go with him. When he came to bring me to the party." She smiled all around. "Sometimes it's best delight to do your shopping when time is running out. It's exciting that way. Yes," she finished. "It is a beautiful purse."

Anna raised her head from the card and the purse. She wished she could say to Uncle Charles, *I love this purse. I'm very sorry.*

But instead she said, "Thank you, Uncle Charles. Thank you again, everybody. Thank you again, very much."

"You're welcome," said Priscilla.

"Now we're all hungry," announced Aunt Eleanor.

"I do the kitchen," said Aunt Maria. "Anna helps."

"I don't," said Priscilla. "Not this year. Anna has

to do my helping, too."

Anna and Aunt Maria walked past the Christmas tree, through the dining room, down the hall, into the kitchen. The kitchen door swung closed behind them.

"Now," said Aunt Maria. "Everything's ready. Everything's ready and waiting. We have only to arrange it into some masterpieces of arranging."

They began work on the masterpieces. On the white kitchen table, Anna set out the serving platters. There were four, from Aunt Eleanor's Christmas set. On the biggest platter, Aunt Maria built a pyramid with the small sandwiches. She went on to the second platter.

"Pickles are hard," she said. "They are so slidey. But aren't the tomato slices pretty with the pickles? Red with the green. That's very nice."

Anna was taking the Christmas cookies—one by one—out of the bakery box.

"The coffee to start," murmured Aunt Maria.

"This is going to be a big cookie snowflake," Anna said. Aunt Maria looked at Anna's snowflake.

"Eleanor doesn't bake cookies," she commented nicely, then added—as though it followed in good sense, "Anna, we have to do the honey cakes beautifully. Aren't you glad we did make them this year!"

Inside the rim of the fourth Christmas platter, Aunt Maria made a brown-and-cream-colored wagon wheel of honey cakes. Anna watched.

Then, in the living room—far away—Aunt Eleanor started to play the piano again. She was playing Christmas carols slowly, just for the music. She was not playing for any singing—the sing-we-all-merrily sort of singing.

The music, not close and not with people's voices singing, suddenly made the honey cakes get blurry for Anna.

Christmas carols are so sad. People forget about Johnny and they sing Christmas carols.

Studying her wheel of honey cakes, Aunt Maria observed, "Honey cakes. It is absolutely a bigger smell than any summer smell."

Windows are open.

Anna's memory furnished that. And it furnished things that happened after that. Anna and Aunt Maria, about to have a Christmas tea party. Having a ring hunt first, and a resting talk near the furnace. It was a talk that was a wonderful present, about Johnny, to Anna, from Aunt Maria. And it stayed that way until the minute when Aunt Eleanor screamed.

And Uncle Charles waited and talked to me. He wouldn't say "Johnny," as though Johnny had done a bad thing by dying, like the baby Kaiser and his crippled arm.

In Aunt Eleanor's kitchen then (with all the masterpieces set out and the smell of coffee beginning and the soft music of Christmas continuing), Anna gulped, and wanted to cry, and said, "Aunt

Maria, they hurt Johnny so much."

In a quiet hurry, without looking up from the honey cakes, Anna told Aunt Maria—about the needles and all the hurt and the kidnaping away of the real Johnny, about her mother's telling the miseries over and over, about the protecting phantom dresses. About her father not being there for any of it.

Maybe it took a long time. Aunt Maria waited without moving. When Anna stopped talking, Aunt Maria put her hands on Anna's shoulders.

"Your poor dear mother, Anna," she said. "She shouldn't do that. She doesn't know she is doing it. And your poor dear father, Anna. Things are not real, at the beginning of grief. Can you believe, Anna—it will stop. Just you endure. It will stop."

"I don't think it will ever stop, Aunt Maria."

"Things stop, Anna. Yes they do. It didn't hurt, after some time, to just dearly remember my mother when she was well—not the way she has been, these last years and years. You will stop needing the dresses for dreaming. And you will just look at my mother's real dresses. The way everyone else looks, liking those dear historical dresses."

The kitchen door swung. They heard it push through the air. They stepped apart.

Anna's mother came into the kitchen. Uncle Charles came, too, right behind her. The next few minutes went rapidly, with everyone talking except Anna.

"You've been back here a long time," Uncle Charles said.

Anna's mother said, sounding vague, "Michael is on Daddy's lap. . . . "

"I'll carry some of the food," said Uncle Charles.

"Yes. But you mustn't disarrange it, Charles," Aunt Maria said.

Anna's mother said, a little more clearly, "I started back, to help."

"You shouldn't have waited so long, there at the door," Uncle Charles said.

The scattered talking stopped.

But Uncle Charles' voice went on. "You should have come right in. Maria dawdles. Everyone's hungry."

Anna's mother said, as though she were thinking it over, making sure it was collected and correct, "I was listening. I was listening to Anna." She added, sure of this: "I am so sorry."

In genuine confusion, without any complaint, Uncle Charles asked, "Sorry? For what?"

"I will tell," said Aunt Maria. In the living room, the Christmas music stopped. Aunt Maria continued, "Rita has needed to talk about Baby Johnny. All the things that hurt him. She talked to Anna. Because Anna was there. And no one else was. Anna's father being alone, too. It is hard for a person to hear things like that, particularly a young person. Because it's terrible, and it frightens a person's insides. They love each other so much, Anna and her mother. They do, Charles. That's why," Aunt Maria finished, "Rita is so sorry. Do you see?"

Uncle Charles answered, "Yes."

The kitchen door swung again. Aunt Eleanor came in. She said, "Priscilla's starving."

Uncle Charles picked up the platter of sandwiches. "Let's get going, then," he said.

They ate in the living room because Priscilla couldn't sit on a dining-room chair.

Aunt Eleanor had folded a blanket on the piano bench and put a green tablecloth over that. The cloth was too large. It spread out on the floor behind the piano bench. But the masterpieces looked good on the green cloth.

"This is an indoor picnic. In the winter," Aunt Eleanor said. "Please help yourselves. Except Priscilla. I'll do hers. Then I'll pass coffee and the children's milk."

Anna sat on the floor near Priscilla, in her present-helper place. She concentrated on eating.

This is what I have to do. Look at food. And eat it.

Everyone ate. It was the proper time for the masterpieces to look messed and jaunty.

"It was all so good, Eleanor," Anna's mother said. The words sounded flat to Anna.

"Tell Maria," said Aunt Eleanor.

"Nonsense," said Aunt Maria happily.

"It's my turn now," said Aunt Eleanor. "I'll clear the dishes."

"No," said Anna's mother. "We'll do it."

Anna started to get up. "Not you, Anna," her mother said. "Daddy."

Anna's father said, "Now that's something I can do."

Anna's parents started to gather away the indoor picnic. She watched them walk toward the kitchen. She thought she saw that, even carrying picnic things, her mother and her father were managing to walk closely together.

She'll be better off with him than with me. Me, in the kitchen, telling Aunt Maria something that should have been a secret. Even from my mother. Especially from my mother.

Michael climbed into Anna's lap.

There wasn't enough time for roundabout talk to start up in the living room before Anna's father returned.

"Last of the dishes," he said to them all. Then he asked, "Do you think, Mikey, that I can clear up the rest of this picnic, with two hands, now? Not have to come back again?"

Michael said, "No."

Priscilla laughed. "Michael, do you ever say yes?" she asked.

"No," said Michael. Priscilla shook her head. Michael leaned against Anna. He was as quiet after that as a little boy full of Christmas could be. Peeking around, Anna saw that his eyes were round and steady.

Aunt Maria was humming. Uncle Charles was

rocking. Aunt Eleanor said, "It turned out to be a good Christmas, after all. You girls deserved it. I'm glad."

There were those small happenings, and a nice absence of talking, for the rest of the time until Anna's parents returned.

Aunt Maria said, "They're back, Charles. We could turn off the lamps now. Just have the fire-light. And the tree. I wish you would. I have a surprise. I'll tell it, with the lamps turned off."

"We always turn them off," Uncle Charles said.

The light was beautifully lessened.

Anna felt numbed by the beauty and by the re-membered sound of her mother saying *I am so sorry*.

She could see a shadowy Michael, now in his fa-ther's arms. She thought she could see that his eyes were closing.

"This is my surprise. I am going to tell about the diamond rings."

Anna could see Aunt Maria smile because Aunt Maria was close to the fireplace and her face was halfway turned to the firelight.

Aunt Eleanor said, "Maria, this is the children's party. Please think about that."

"I've thought about it for a long time," Aunt Maria said. "Two rings are for Priscilla. And she will give one to her mother. Everyone has to be sensible about diamonds. I'll wear them myself for a while. While I want to. And one ring," declared

Aunt Maria, "is for Anna. Because she is family. When the girls," she finished triumphantly, "are older."

"What can a person say?" asked Aunt Eleanor.

"Merry Christmas," suggested Aunt Maria.

"Wow!" said Priscilla.

"Michael's asleep," murmured Anna's father.

Uncle Charles turned on the piano lamp. It was as far away from Michael as any lamp in the room could be.

Everyone was quiet as the party ended.

"I'll come over with you," said Uncle Charles. "I'll push the shovel ahead, for a path. It will be a blizzard by now. You have to watch your step, carrying Michael."

"You won't mind leaving your presents for tonight, will you, Anna?" her mother asked softly.

"She can carry the purse," Aunt Maria offered. "I'll fetch a bag."

It was a blue-and-white striped bag. Aunt Maria brought it very close to Anna while Anna's mother was trying to button Michael's coat. Aunt Maria held the bag elaborately open for the purse. She bowed her head over the bag and whispered, "At home, Anna. Look in the bottom of the bag."

She raised her head. "Anna does like her purse, Charles," she said. "Sometime you should put a penny in it for her. For good luck."

"Yes," said Uncle Charles. "For good luck."

In an accident of timing then, Anna looked at

Uncle Charles, and Uncle Charles looked at Anna. The accident lasted only part of a minute, Anna was sure.

In that time Uncle Charles said—gently, "For grown-up luck, maybe a dime. The girls are growing up—Anna, faster."

And Anna said, comfortably, "A penny's fine, Uncle Charles." The time ended, having been fine itself.

Uncle Charles shrugged on his coat.

Aunt Maria whispered happily, "Charles! A dime. That's charming."

Charming.

The word descended on Anna. It was something she could have shared with her mother. She could have used this *charming* to add to the Uncle Charles things she and her mother had talked nicely about. She could have reported something new and surprising and good that she had discovered about Uncle Charles: that he could understand one thing (and maybe more) about Priscilla's friend—who was really Anna Halder.

But I can't now. What kind of way can my mother and I talk to each other now?

Fifteen

Uncle Charles pushed his shovel across Hunt Street. Anna's mother followed next. Anna's father carried Michael.

In the middle of the street, Anna looked up from her careful walking and saw Michael open his eyes. She saw the streetlight reflected in the centers of Michael's dark eyes, two white buttons there. Then the snow blew, and Michael closed the buttons away and snuggled down again.

Uncle Charles cleared their front steps. Uncle Charles gave Michael a pat. Uncle Charles pushed his shovel home.

Michael was completely asleep when Anna's mother carried him up the stairs.

That left Anna and her father together in the front hall. He said, "Merry Christmas, Anna." He put his arm around her shoulder. He kissed her cheek. "I'm glad that we were with everyone tonight, aren't you, Anna? And we have our own Christmas tomorrow, coming. Special . . ." He hugged a little tighter before stepping away. Then he smiled—a come-and-go smile, happy and sad. "Christmas keeps its promise, if you let it, I guess," he said, almost whispering.

"I guess so. I guess so, too, Daddy."

Now her father smiled, a real smile. "It's a good guess we just guessed here, Anna. Probably no one before us ever guessed it."

"You're teasing, Daddy."

"How did you guess?"

"Smart," answered Anna. "Merry Christmas, Daddy."

"Sleep tight, Anna, good guesser."

Anna liked that—the silly, comfortable fun of being a good guesser.

She took two steps up the staircase, and couldn't hold on to the fun. Then and immediately, she had to remember Aunt Eleanor's kitchen. Her mother saying, "I am so sorry."

Almost frightened, Anna hurried to get into bed.

In the black bedroom, she kept hoping that her mother would decide, "Anna is probably asleep by now. I won't go in."

I can't talk to my mother tonight. It's too soon.

It wasn't a possible hope. Her mother came in. She began by saying, in the dark, "We should have brought the red-and-green rug. Merry Christmas, Anna."

She sat down on the bed. "Aunt Maria was talking just now about Grandmother's rings, wasn't she? I know she was, and I do know what she said. But that wasn't important. The important thing was to keep thinking about what to say to you." There was a silence that seemed long. Then she went on, very slowly. "Anna, I didn't know that I was hurting you."

I can't cry now. That wouldn't be fair. By the time you were talking, I was making princess dresses, not having to think about Johnny.

"Anna, I want you to let me tell you something else. I'll tell it like a story—because that will be easier for me. Like telling you little-girl stories that weren't long either. Anna, once there was a mother saying to a father, 'Please talk to me about Johnny.' And the father crying and saying, 'I can't talk about Johnny.'"

"Daddy," Anna whispered.

"The mother went to the next person and didn't ask anything. She just talked there, without knowing." Her mother took Anna's hand. "I didn't know I was talking to you. I do think that is how it happened. Aunt Maria was right, about all of us. I told Daddy, there in Eleanor's kitchen."

Daddy. Making it better. Teasing about guessing.

Anna sat up. She and her mother hugged. And now they did cry. Both of them cried, with just a little noise.

At some point, Anna said, in tears, "We can remember things about Johnny, Mother. Not in the hospital."

"Anna . . . "

"I know we can, Mother. I know how. You and I and Daddy can. He wants to. I know."

"When we're all settled. When we're not crying . . . "

In time, the crying was finished. The hug lasted longer.

Finally, Anna's mother stood. She said faintly but with no sadness, "The merry part of this Christmas went wandering before it got here, didn't it, Anna?"

"I think Aunt Maria followed it and caught it," Anna said shakily.

"Aunt Maria. On a horse, I suppose you see her? Or on a little donkey?"

"Just walking," Anna answered. "Waving. With her rings sparkling."

"Anna dear, don't wait for diamonds. I know you won't. Although Aunt Maria meant it tonight."

"I won't wait," said Anna. "A person has to be sensible about diamonds."

Her mother laughed, the little pleasant sound that stops with itself and doesn't go on to be anything more, not even a chuckle.

"Good night, Anna dear."

At the door of Anna's room, on her way out, Anna's mother automatically reached over and flipped the light switch up. In the second before she flipped it down, yellow light jumped out and flared.

Anna sat up in bed, an instant big-eyed jack-in-the-box.

"Why did I do that!" her mother said.

She walked out of the dark room. She closed the door. Anna could still see a yellow flare, the experience of a yellow flare. She could still see, in that yellow, Aunt Maria's bag on the floor near her desk. Anna brought the bag, in the dark, up to her desk. She felt the purse and took it out.

Now how do I look in the bottom of the bag? Merry Christmas, Anna Halder! Turn on your desk lamp!

At the bottom was a gift bag, not large, white with a printed gold ribbon. The gift was in a box that said "Harold Anderson. Fine Jewelry."

It was a silver bracelet. A chain bracelet with small links. The links were regular circles at both ends, moving on toward the middle. The links in the middle were more solid, but just as small.

Anna held the bracelet under the desk lamp. The center links said "ANNE IS ELEGANT."

Aunt Maria's writing on the gift card was nearly as small and neat as that.

Say it is from someone who made a mistake, if you wish. I shopped in the snow today. People were so accommodating. Mr. Anderson, we've known him for years, had the right letters in his store. He had more letters than usual because it's Christmas. I picked the most secret ones. Dear Anna.

"Dear Aunt Maria."

Anna looked steadily at the secret letters in her hand. Tomorrow morning, when they were opening family presents, she would be wearing the bracelet.

Michael would say, "I want to see, Anna."

Her parents would ask, "What does it mean, Anna?"

It means that Aunt Maria told me about a name like Wisteria trailing along behind a funny little girl. Her parents would nod and smile. *"Maria."*

Later, when Michael was napping, *with my big-smiley-mouse present under the covers, too,* Anna would talk about Grandmother's funeral day. The stubborn diamond ring and Mrs. Simpson's husbands and Mrs. Parrot. Her mother and father would like that a lot. *Oh, it all sounds like Maria, over and over! Doesn't it just!*

Then . . . *"We're not crying now, Anna."* Maybe her mother would say that on Christmas afternoon.

She will say it sometime. I'll be able to tell about Johnny—remembering Johnny things.

Anna stretched high, the bracelet closed in her hand. Her mouth stretched in a serious closed smile. A major big-mouth yawn took over.

Anna put everything back in the blue-and-white bag just the way Aunt Maria had arranged it. She replaced the bag, and turned out her desk lamp.

In bed again, she was sure she was going to fall asleep fast. But instead, she thought—with every detail clear as print—about wearing the elegant bracelet one certain time.

On the bus. On the way to the historical society. Leo McVene with her on the bus. Saying, "I like the historical society."

Anna saying, "And we go to Aunt Maria's, right after."